In Love With

A

Siren

Written by Paul Kuipa

In Love With A Siren

Paul Kuipa

Published by Paul Kuipa, 2021.

While every precaution has been taken in the preparation of this book, the publisher assumes no responsibility for errors or omissions, or for damages resulting from the use of the information contained herein.

IN LOVE WITH A SIREN

First edition. December 11, 2021.

Copyright © 2021 Paul Kuipa.

ISBN: 979-8201834258

Written by Paul Kuipa.

Preface
INTRODUCTION
CHAPTER ONE
CHAPTER TWO
CHAPTER THREE
CHAPTER FOUR
CHAPTER FIVE
CHAPTER SIX
CHAPTER SEVEN
Chapter Eight
CHAPTER NINE
CHAPTER TEN
CHAPTER ELEVEN
CHAPTER TWELVE
CHAPTER THIRTEEN

Preface

Mermaids exists whether you believe it or you do not. People assume that stories about mermaids are actually a harbinger of doom. Don't believe the Disney hype about mermaids being sweet fish-women seeking their soul mate. In reality, we characterize sinister mermaids as sea-monsters, a creature with half body human and half fish. Christians they call it demons, women that had sexual intimacy with Angels and bear great giants during the ancient time of Noah. God destroyed them with the floods and their spirits became water spirits. In Zimbabwe the call them (njuzu) which means mermaids. They said to take the form of a whirlwind in order to travel to the land. That's why elders said don't run into whirlwinds or storms, mermaids can capture you. Mermaids don't want fragrance cosmetics and also they don't want to be spotted, they will attack you. Once they take you, they will confuse you mind, some it's food have worms but you will forget that worms shouldn't be eaten. They will never allow to return a person they take with no ritual performed.

Within the lore and history of actual sightings of mermaids and various merbeings all over the world, these creatures have come in a surprisingly wide array of forms. There are the beautiful maidens of legend with their flowing hair and fishtails, the more ape-like fish beasts of other traditions, and pretty much everything in between. Dispositions range all over the place as well, with merbeings running the gamut from seductive sirens, to benevolent protectors of the sea, to shy and reclusive things only fleetingly seen, to vicious, savage monsters that can only be described as sinister and evil. Of the many places from which merbeings are reported, one place that definitely has the latter is the continent of Africa. Here on the Dark Continent, "mermaids" are considered being far from mere legend and also seem to be rather far from benevolent. Many regions of Africa have a rich tradition of mermaids, particularly in the southern portion of the continent. In the country of Zimbabwe mermaids have long featured prominently in various myths and legends, where they are often called the Mondao and are portrayed as malicious creatures that enjoy pulling bathers or swimmers under the waves to their death.

Although many sees such tales as just spooky lore, there are quite a few Zimbabweans who believe that they actually exist, and incidents or sightings involving mermaids often crop up here. For example: Some work being carried out at the Gokwe dam in the Midlands and the Osborne dam in Manicaland, on reservoirs near the towns of Gokwe, Manicaland, and Mutare, was suspended because workers refused to go to work because they claimed to have been terrorized by the mermaids lurking there, which were said to look like pale-skinned humans with black hair and fish tails. Many stories about them, as I was attacked by mermaids before, so I write this book based on a true story, exposing the dark secrets of mermaids. I hope you will all enjoy the contents of this book.

INTRODUCTION

Running alongside the Mozambican border for some 300 kilometers, the Eastern Highlands is mountainous area of spectacular natural beauty: rolling hills, green forests, rugged peaks, misty valleys, deep gorges, cascading waterfalls, and sparkling rivers and lakes. This is a totally different side to Zimbabwe that most visitors know: the cool damp climate and lush green landscapes of the Eastern Highlands are a contrast to the dry savanna in other parts of the country. While there is some game in the parks of the highlands, this is not a prime safari destination. Instead, people visit the Eastern Highlands for the outdoors activities of hiking, horse riding, fishing and golf, and the superb bird life and the stunning scenery.

The Eastern Highlands is made up of three areas—the Nyanga Highlands in the north, the Vumba Mountains in the center and the Chimanimani Mountains in the south—each of which has its own attractions. In the rolling hills of the north, Nyanga National Park is where you'll find Zimbabwe's highest mountain, Mount Nyangani, and its highest waterfall, Mtazari Falls as well as wildlife, lots of birds, wonderful hiking trails and excellent trout fishing. The central highlands are home to the city of Mutare—the biggest settlement in the region—but the real draw is the Vumba Mountains, where lush forests are home to rare bird species and the Samango monkey. In the southern highlands, Chimanimani National Park is excellent for mountain hiking, while you can indulge in some forest therapy at Chirinda Forest Reserve, Africa's most southern tropical rainforest, and go horseback riding in the hills.

Its mysteries

The breathtaking scenery and plentitude of wildlife have made the park one of Zimbabwe's premiere tourist attractions and sitting at the center of this entire natural splendor to dominate the surrounding landscape is the majestic Mount Nyangani. At 2,592 meters (8,504 ft.) high, it is the highest point in Zimbabwe, and its plateau of moorland, steep drops, and seemingly eternally mist capped peaks give it a rather imposing, mysterious appearance, and it is also known for dramatic weather changes at a moment's notice, which all makes it perhaps not a surprise that legends have orbited it for centuries. In local tradition, Mount Nyangani is inhabited by powerful ancestral spirits and is a sacred place. It is also said to be the haunt of evil or vindictive spirits and all manner of supernatural entities and creatures. The mountain has long been feared by the people of the region, a place to be approached with caution, and there are numerous rules that according to lore must be followed when venturing there. One is not to approach or enter sacred locations upon the mountain, for it is said to do so will result in becoming hopelessly lost and unable to leave, doomed to aimlessly wander the mountain unless the angered spirits responsible are appeased somehow. It is also said that if one comes across a colorful snake, a pot with no fire, or a brick of gold it is the spirits tricking you, and that you had better ignore them and quickly move on. The same mischievous spirits are said to enjoy pushing people from steep ledges, with varied advice on ways to avoid their wrath, such as refraining from urinating on the mountain, avoiding profanity, and by all means abstaining from any sort of sexual activity.

It is also recommended not to wear red clothing, as this apparently greatly upsets the spirits. Even if one plans to follow these set rules, visitors are strongly implored to seek permission from the village elders of the area before embarking These are the dark rumors and legends that have been whispered about among local tribes since time unremembered, but if the phenomena associated with this place are anything to go on, there is something more at work here than just pure folklore. Visitors and locals who have come to the mysterious mountain have experienced a wide range of strangeness. It is said that compasses and electrical equipment will sometimes go haywire or break down entirely here, and that sometimes photos taken here will not develop properly. The weather is reported as almost having a malevolent mind of its own, with gusts of wind seeming to roar in at the most inopportune times and thick fogs or mists that materialize out of nowhere to follow hikers around as if stalking them. There are also numerous reports of visitors becoming dazed, confused, or disoriented for no apparent reason, with even experienced hikers familiar with the area at times becoming hopelessly lost, as well as sudden bouts of profound dizziness or nausea that pass as abruptly as they come. Other various weirdness are unidentifiable sounds, strange lights, and animals that seem to watch and follow visitors around, as well as trees that are twisted into the visage of human faces and talk or whisper, or streams that suddenly turn a blood red in color.

Even the area surrounding the mountain is saturated with spooky lore telling of magical locations and strange beasts. Close to this mountain lays our village, Dombo village. Not crowded but richer in minerals and vegetation.

CHAPTER ONE

There was a water hole at our residence which never goes dry throughout the year and turned into a great blessing to the people living in Dombo village. Most communities in our area obtain their water from this waterhole, which was capable of holding enormous volumes of freshwater. All people came to fetch water, young and old age especially youthful and young girls. Ladies were the oftenest to visit this well, not only females but pretty ones. But to me that was not my style being attentive or proposing to girls. I had no colleagues. Even my best buddies I used to hang up with ditched me. They claimed I was blocking them with discomfort and make them sick because of my toxic behavior of not interested in ladies. And our friendship quickly turned toxic because I was varied from them. They loved hanging around with girls and I wasn't. Honestly speaking, because of the many stories I have heard before, I discovered that people who fell in the name of love and respected it, that same love contributed to their downfall. What I am asserting is that many cultures have considered romantic love to be a crucial factor in achieving personal fulfillment and a peaceful life. However, erotic love is also a major cause of misery, as it contains many regrets and unfulfilled hopes. Love may be wonderful and fill our hearts with joy, but love also hurts a lot and can be dangerous, leading us to unwise actions.

That's what caused fear in me to be permanent when it comes to women. I am a 19-year-old boy. We were in the month of August, the time of the spring, the breezy month, when wind greets concrete and skin just the same. Its giddy currents flow through woodland canopies, shacks, unaware of how its song soothes those who can hear. With its coldness and rushing wind, the implements of July. As an individual who was jobless, I usually wakes up and sat outside the house sunbathing though people said you will have cancer because of the excess sun, frankly I always worshipped the sun. Mostly I will start having conversations with people who come to the well because I was one of a kind of person who likes socializing with people. Quite frankly, that was my daily routine of my everyday life. One day, I woke up and rumbled to my guard-post as usual. And the artistic golden sun got up like a baby and started painting the dark black sky into a bright blue sky.

The bright lucking milky clouds act up from sleep and start travelling around the sky, visiting the surrounding. There comes a beautiful, charming young lady at the well to fetch water. It was my first time lusting to a woman, feeling my heart thudding so fast at a rapid pace. Genuinely she was gorgeous. I adored her curves of softness. With the muscle of a footballer and the blessed fat of a baby, she was the most astonishing girl I ever met... She had safe eyes, perhaps that's the best way to express it. She had a beauty that made those billboards-princesses look as paper thin as they are; she was something robust and real... though didn't even greeted me, my eyes kept fastened on her body observing her structure from top to bottom with a withering stare. Once her bucket was full, she carried it on her head then started going. She was adorable; of course I will name a star after her once she say i do... I told myself. As I was left behind speechless, My brain stutters for a moment and my eyes take in more light than I expected, every part of me goes on pause while my thoughts catch up. After a wash of cold I step from the shadows, her beauty blinded me. I followed her sneaking behind to the point to see which house she was going. She walked so elegantly, her hair glided through the wind, her body moved to the beat of his heart. She went inside a nearby house, then I returned home being jovial and I felt my conscience that she is the one going to complete my life.

The next day I was ready for her, once she comes back again, it was the perfect time to propose. I will not let this magical moment slipping away from my fingers. I started pacing back and forth at the waterhole clenched my hands inside my pockets. I was practicing what i had seen all the time in those romance movies. But how did someone go about doing that? Will I just go on my knees and go, "will you marry me?", or wait for someone to talk first on my behalf? There were so many questions left unanswered, all of which left my heart hammering in my chest, but the biggest question for me was, will she even say yes? Speaking of the devil, in the midst of my thoughts she came with her bucket straight to where I was. She turned to look at me and we greeted each other and told her some funny stories at first before going to the point. I was sweating, it was obvious, but i didn't care, it was my moment of Bravado. When she was about to go i rapidly hold her hands kneeling on the ground. Her eyes widened and her mouth gaped as I sputtered, "I love you, and want to spend the rest of my life with you. Will you marry me?". Beloved ones, it was a steep mountain to climb to win her heart, almost a month passed by, but I didn't give up until I won her heart. Her name was Rosemary. She was very good to me, a breathtaking, enchanting girl. What about her skin, structure and glowed gleaming eyes? I am out of words mmm. We fall in lavatorial love, a free flowing relationship that wanted not to miss each other. Any time I was available no matter what time because of being unemployed. When holiday passed, Rosemary refused to go back and told her sister that she wanted to start a new school here.

To me, I was available at any time. Rosemary was also young with only 16 years. One day, I asked Rosemary to come and let us spend the whole day together while my sister was away and I was left alone.

She came in the morning and locked her up the whole day inside the house. We chatted and chatted, knowing each other better.

Rosemary told me, her parents were all dead. She was living with her grandmother in Masvingo. Here in Dombo she was on vacation to see her sister. I also lived with my sister, who kept and took care of me since from the death of our parents. Our home was a nice place, a mansion itself. Our house was the result of years of hard labor. At the height of its sumptuousness, it was the jewel of the river; People assumes maybe we used (muti) charms to become prosperous and they added that maybe our house was built using blood money because it does not deserve to be built in rural areas only suburbs.. My sister was working in UK so it was orderly organized and I was living with my brother Prince only. I told Rosemary that my parents are alive, stays in Johannesburg in South Africa. So this house is all mine and is built in my name. , A man who lie doesn't can't marry you know especially when it comes to impress the ladies. To me lies slips out, smoothly and easily like melted butter running down toast. We spend the whole day until around four pm when Rosemary said she was starving and need chips. Even if a lady asks you for a snake, no matter how hard it is, you will find a way to bring her that snake.

I was having a few coins in my pocket; I took those and went straight to a tuck-shop nearby to get her chips. On my way out, I meet with Prince on his way home. I told her to accompany Rosemary until my arrival. Running was in my veins and blood, I pounded my feet across the road, as my lungs strained instead of spending twenty more minutes I take only less than ten minutes, I was back with hot chips breathing heavily, showing signs of exhaustion playing its factor. Opening the door, I was welcomed by water flooding on its way out to the entrance. It was flooding the whole floor. Prince was standing on top of the couch in awe, covering his mouth with hands. His heart was nearly to leap out from his chest, forcing himself to stand despite being wrapped with fear. "Leave it brother, come and sit here?" he was pointing his fingers the couch. But instead I sat next to Rosemary whose face was long and serious. I looked her with a talking eye saying *what did Prince do to you, babe?* I looked again at Prince, whom his pulse was pounding in his ears and being puzzled at the same time. This made my heart to thud louder and louder at a fast pace and felt that something was not right. Water kept flowing, and I went outside to check maybe there was a leakage or something which is causing water oozing inside like this but there was nothing. Prince followed me and said that he was going out for a walk to clear his head which was in a Dracula wheel situation.

I rumbled back inside the house and caught by a huge surprise, Rosemary was laying on the floor in the water, rolling, twisting and turning like a snake. Which made my gut to twist what is this now? Shock registered on my face, I tried to lift her up on her feet but I felt power withdrawn from me and froze for an instant, a slight headache felt upon me... Bang... I fell on the ground though I tried to stand on my feet but something invisible kept pinned my body to the ground so I could not move a muscle, only rolling my eyes watching my beloved wife doing fish abilities. Couple of minutes passed by being on the ground bang! Bang! Bang!!!!! A huge knock at the door. Quickly I stood up and opened the door to see who this person with this kind of knock was. Another surprise, Rosemary's relatives were crowded outside in anger holding weapons in their hands as if they were going to the battlefield to face a deadly enemy. Panic rose like bile in my body, the real surprise is when the wish unexpected comes true. "Goo.. d. Evening" I mumbled.

CHAPTER TWO

They stood in mute mode as if they were missing ears. I knew that I was in trouble. One ought never to turn ones back on a threatened danger and try to run away from it. If you go on with that, you will double the danger. But if you meet it promptly and without flinching, you will reduce the danger by half. Never run away from anything. Never! Quickly, I closed the door halfway point distracting their view inside the house. What a brilliant act from Mr. Genius. Rosemary then rose from the floor to the couch glaring petulant through the window where raging angry mob launched, full of energy, the kind that causes fear bubbling beneath your skin and vibrates right down to the bones. This type of energy was contagious. You can literally feel and hear the high voltage zinging through all the people. Prince arrived to worsening the situation by walking past through the crowd, so disrespectful cantankerous. Stubbornly obstructive and unwilling to cooperate, then stood at the entrance starring the crowd. What a quality possessed by Prince who tends to take risks. "Hey you bunch of morons, who gave you that…, this nasty permission of jumping at my fence as if there is no gate?" Huh! He said bravely waiting for an answer. That's the act of a damn person who doesn't like people to get in his shoes, but not on this situation. What I only saw, my beloved brother being dragged inside the mob and started receiving the worst beating they think he deserves. I watched him pleading for his life, his body straining every muscle to express his desperation, his intense desire to live. His hands clawed at the earth, as if somehow he could just dig his way out and escape the fate.

He let out a scream of anguish and felt my gut clench as the hopelessness of the situation sank in. Tears broke seeing him being beaten up like this, though I craved to help but I saw that they outnumbered us. I ran inside, took Rosemary and locked her inside the bedroom then rushed back to the door and stand firm. The moment I arrived was just the same time Prince was jumping the yard fence being chased. My brother, I knew so extremely well, once scared he lost all rationality and became a monster that would do anything to survive. Once saw that they failed to catch him, they all returned to me with their wrath being aroused. "Are you sure to spend the whole day sleeping with our child as if you paid the dowry? You are lunatic and you will see us today" said the woman who charging at me "Your child is not here. Please trust me if you don't believe you may come inside and look for yourself" I remarked calmly. As their frustration builds in and about to explode, they pushed me away from the entrance as they were entering. They left me at the door as they were busy doing the searching, some were even calling Rosemary to come out by herself before they find her. Should I run away from my home? I asked myself if I could really get beaten at my place. It will be an embarrassment.

"Go get the bedroom keys from him" hearing their voices talking to each other about keys; this injected a very effective dosage of fear into my system. I only jumped the outside fence because the gate was too far. I could only hear my heels clicking, hitting the pavement running towards mountains. They tried to chase me but they only saw dust left behind as a faithful witness to my disappearance in thin air. I wonder of the perspective of the chasers, if they can fathom the fear of the chased. For in this need to escape my head and heart go to the place that is crushed and without light or match to bring a comforting spark. I feel the screaming of my lungs and the will of my muscles to go far beyond what exercise could ever demand. This is the body and brain if full survival mode. I hid underneath a small cave trying to catch my breath by breathing in and out but air won't enter my lungs for a while, starved for air my heart raced tremendous speeds. As sunset arrived, the sun dipped below the horizon, the fleeting colors of dusk began to fade away. The charcoal-black rocks circles around the mountain, shimmering confidently before dark fell upon them.

Today I survived through the fingertips of the enemies but I knew that the battle was not yet over. My brain had shut down in fear. I was clammy and there was the glisten of a cold sweat. My eyes were wide as if someone was coming to deliver the fatal blow. Trapped in my own psychosis, a living nightmare of being caught. A tailor made by my own brain to play on my deepest fear. Past seven, past eight still in the mountain both scared of the dark and worried about Rosemary. *I locked her up in the bedroom and keys are with me, what she would do?* This drove me to climb down from the mountain and started going home. I was walking slowly, listening carefully that nobody was following me. The darkness was as thick as I walked down the road and trees looked nothing they do in the daylight. It was though everything disappeared and suddenly the world closed in and became tiny. I sneaked inside our yard without the act of not being seen. When entered the yard zone, the silence put me on edge; It was about as normal as deserted streets in Zimbabwe's rush-hour. Even the birds had ceased to sing. I looked through the window inside the house; the light was switched off as well. Slow and deliberate, I turned the door handle, and I was in. I walked across the room and stopped abruptly in the middle; I kicked something but couldn't tell what it was. I switched the light and saw it was a big bag dropped on the floor. Guess whose clothes were inside? Who brought Rosemary's clothes here? A gaggle of goose pimples laminated my frigid, naked skin. It mixed me up and Prince was not back yet after being chased. I unlocked the bedroom's door.

Rosemary was seated at the edge of the bed. "Babe, who brought your clothes here? To do what? Wake up, let's go to your house now it's late" I asked all these questions at the same time to a single person and waited to be answered but no one answered until a moment of silence passed. "My sister is the one who brought my clothes here and urges me not to come back home anymore, so what you are saying is nothing." *What?* I tried to persuade her to go, but she refused wholeheartedly. Me with my age to be called a married man? Hell no. I was left speechless, not knowing what to do next. I went outside for a moment to clear my head maybe I was hallucinating but when I came back the results was still the same. Rosemary was already inside the blankets. I sat at the edge of the bed, another thought was saying, *call your sister now and tell her all this!* The other was saying *wait until tomorrow.*

First day, first love and for the first time... I jumped inside the blankets and started romancing my newly wife with this feeling of a singular and intense experience that many young teens hope to experience. My brown eyes started caterwauling as soon as i lifted her. She leaped out of my grip and trotted off to the back door entering Patricia's room without a backward glance, followed by me. When it was time for the real game to begin, Rosemary was plain. Mysteriously. Meaning there was no private organ on Rosemary. I tried very hard but to no avail to find it, as my first time I thought it was my fault that's why I was failing to find it. Even asking her, where I should start, I will embarrass myself in front of her. I shoot cum on her thighs and fell asleep. That day I dreamt being fish as well as Rosemary, swimming, it was fun because I was enjoying the spotlight. Rosemary was trying to get out of the dam and started suffocating. And I would come to her rescue then went back inside the deep waters, again and again. As we were still swimming, I was distracted from my dreams by the alarmed of my phone, which nearly burst my eardrums in halves. I woke up realizing that I was wet. When I opened my eyes, it was still dark, half asleep. I got out of the bed and entered the bathroom. As I emptied my bladder, I checked my face in the mirror. For an instant, I could recognize the person reflected in it. Only when I waved back that I realized it was me. When I was back to the bedroom, there was water again on the floor, everywhere? I felt as though I had entered a house with the gas stove on; the atmosphere was dense and strange as well as outside.

Misty and fog was scattered everywhere to the extent that our gate was invisible. I was stunned because in the water were pieces of fresh green reeds in it. I stood there for what felt like an eternity but was actually only two minutes. This was too much for me; I went to the dining room and threw myself on the couch confused. Rosemary came and learns by the door staring at me with a strong love smile, which made me feel powerless. "Good morning, Daddy," she said sitting next to me, wrapping her hands around my waist. "Nigel, you seemed troubled. What is eating you up, darling?" She remarked calmly. I lied to that I was just worried about Prince. But where he was since yesterday. Thoughts came about what happened last night and I came to her wanted to have sex with her. I said to myself that I was going to have a clean conversation with her. I was so casual about that. I started to forget everything and that love sensation grew in me. We started kissing again and throw her on the bed. I was now riding the high of love, my smile met with my ears and with that warm, tingly feeling in the pit of my stomach. But as I was on the downside of the rush, it feels more like a thousand burning needles to the heart (um, maybe a big of an exaggeration, but not by much!) I just took off the top and.....

CHAPTER THREE

She leaned forward, took my head then in her hands, and kissed me. Oh God I was like in Paris, I put my arms close around her. Prince showed up and spoiled everything, did he? Yes he did, I was about to make love with my charming new partner. As an amateur, this woman's stuff I was having a zero idea about it, in fact zero knowledge though I needed to ask Prince, but was afraid to embarrass myself asking these types of questions. Rosemary quickly stood up and went into the dining room and greeted Prince. Prince saw something on Rosemary that period I left them and went to the shops for chips.

So he asked me to go out for a private discussion, but Rosemary insisted to let me go because she answered she still needed space to spend alone with her spouse. Prince went out, leaving us two alone. I took my phone and broke the good news to my aunt who lived in Harare that I am now married. She was so excited and can't stop looking forward to see Rosemary. The next day around ten in the morning she arrived from Harare to here it's a long distance and a lot of ground to cover. Oh, was she flying? She was in love with both Rosemary's body and soul. Her temperament is what lures me into her also. Her deep soothing voice is what I crave for and her warmth is what I covet. When she smiles at me it seems as if the whole world is mine. When our eyes exchange looks it feels as if everything has paused and belongs right in its place. Her mesmerizing oceanic eyes have locked themselves in my mind and only thoughts about her mingled in my head. She loved her at first sight to the extent of refusing to leave her. It was only for a week, so I granted my Aunty permission to do not argue and left her mother-in-law with her have a great time.

Once they had gone, I lay on my bed then went to sleep. Again the same dream of being fish repeated itself; luckily I was saved from this nightmare by a phone call. "Shit," I said to myself. "What was that nightmare about? Good thing it was only a dream."

I wiped the sweat off my forehead and sat up on my bed. It was Rosemary who wanted to tell me she had arrived in Harare. When I finished talking on the phone, Prince came and sat next to me and began to question me. Prince "What happened to Rosemary first day she started coming here?" Me: "Mm Nothing. What did you see?" Prince: 'Ah, when you went to buy some chips, she told me every secret about our family. The death of parents I mean everything. But why you Nigel told her all about our family. Is it love?" Me: ""I said nothing to her only said that our parents were alive. Just tell me Prince you made gossip to Rosemary about our family and now you are putting the blame on me. " We argued blaming each other about family secrets to Rosemary. Prince: "But how is your wife?" **Me:** "What do you mean by that?'"

Prince: "That very day she said that she got up from the sofa and jumped over here down to the floor and started rolling, twisting like a snake or a fish. It was weird and hard to watch, after water began to emerge when she was lying on the floor.

That's the water you saw which was filled the entire room mmm. Something is not right on your wife. "

I did not want to reply him anymore enough drama. When you're stressed, moving isn't always as simple as it sounds. I felt a lot of tension in my neck and shoulders. When and once those muscles seized up, it doesn't take much for that to turn into a spasm or a full-on pulled muscle. Though it was hard, I got up and went to the bedroom and lay on my back stressed and shocked about what Prince told me. Plus, my dream and how I woke up water being everywhere. It all disappeared when Rosemary wiped my face. *What is going on?* I asked myself but nobody answered me. *Plus yesterday, I failed to have sex with her because of her private organ, which was nowhere to be found.* A splash of stress strikes me again. Lastly, I jumped into conclusion that maybe it was my ancestors who was refusing the bride... This day Sleep came like the falling of an axe. I knew with all this stressful moments it should come but I fought it with everything that I have. Those defenseless hours, oblivious to my surroundings weren't enough to light up my whole body with fiery sparks. I am utterly wired until that time when I cannot fight it anymore and the sleep is as instantaneous as it is unwelcome. I had some warning though, when my thoughts become intertwined with random ideas, impossible ideas, and stressful questions. My phone which ranged so loudly awakened me from my dream land. I got up and took the phone and guess what! Six missed calls on it from auntie. Oh, maybe it was Rosemary who was already missing me, I thought.

I came out from the blankets and put my phone in my pocket and went outside to refresh myself. Just at the door it ranged again suddenly got a glimpse, and it was a call from aunt again. I looked for a place where I can sit comfortably and sat so I can talk to my babe nicely. **Me:** 'Hello sweetheart" **Caller:** Nigel, Nigel, Nigel come here and take your wife today. Do you hear me? **Me** "What happened aunt? You said Sunday after seven days" **Caller:** "No, no, no, no Nigel come today not Sunday it's far. Why didn't you tell me the truth before I take her? You got nerves really, come now please be fast. ''what's the rush? Immediately cut off the call and thought carefully, w*hat aunt was trying to say? We agreed Sunday. What happened and why she said I got balls, what did I do?* Whilst in the middle of battling with my mind. She called again. "Nigel, are you in a taxi now? Fast my son. "

Me: What? I don't have any money. What's all the rush? Did Rosemary did anything wrong?" **Caller:** "Don't ask me so many questions. Find someone to borrow you money I will give you back that money here. Nigel my son. " Phone hung up, I quickly rushed inside the house wiped my face and put on my grown-up, big boy clothes which never quite fitting. Oh God feeling dwarf. And grabbed my pocket which was having few coins, straight to the taxis. Luckily, there was a tax that was only left with one person. Within an hour, I was in Harare and alight the taxi straight to aunt's house in Kuwadzana, one of the biggest locations in Harare. I didn't tell Prince that I was going to Harare with the doors swished opened.

At the gate, what surprised me to see was, i saw Rosemary and Auntie coming from the shops holding together a plastic bag with food, seemed to be on the same page, laughing together so hard. As happy as a baboon in a banana tree. As happy as a clam at high tide. As happy as a hippo in mud. As happy as a shark in a shoal of sea bream. As happy as a kitty in a cream pie. As happy as a dog at a dinosaur dig. She even bought Rosemary new clothes which fitted her. Once I saw her in this her eyes, which cast the brilliancy of emeralds, were perfectly beautiful, and yet were at the same time full of sweetness and majesty. Her mouth was small and rosy; and although she under lip, like that of all princes of the House of Austria, protruded slightly beyond the other, it was eminently lovely in its smile, but as profoundly disdainful in its contempt. Her skin was admired for its velvety softness; her hands and arms were of surpassing beauty, all the poets of the time singing them as incomparable.

Lastly, her hair, which, from being light in her youth, had become chestnut, and which she wore curled very plainly, and with much powder, admirably set off her face, in which the most rigid critic could only have desired a little less rouge, and the most fastidious sculptor a little more fineness in the nose. I felt proud coming inside me and boastful that indeed I was having a good choice to choose Rosemary.

Once her eyes set on me, instantly she jumped out of joy and ran to me, pulled me closer to her wrapping her arms around me. Her embrace was warm, and her small softy arms seemed very protective and caring when wrapped around my frail body. The world around me melted away as I squeezed her back, not wanting the moment to end. We were already missed each other with a single day as if it's ten years without seeing each other. Auntie arrived where we were and greeted me with all the happiness and we went inside the house. Auntie and Rosemary were talking and laughing to each other like what a mother and her daughter did. To me I was eager to hear what i was called here for. Rosemary finished cooking, we ate and Auntie called me outside for a private conversation and Rosemary left washing dishes. **Auntie:** "Nigel, my son tells me more about Rosemary." **Me:** "What do you want to hear about her auntie?" **Auntie:** Why did you hurry to tell her our family secrets? Then to tell her all the names of all the relatives who have died, was it only stories to talk Nigel?"

Me: "Ah, I did not tell her mom all these I told her my mom and daddy is alive. Nothing more about our family secrets. " **Auntie:** "My son, your wife, is very strange. No family member she did not mention about. Every single unmarried person she asked wondering why they were not married. She asked me some deceased family names at our rural home that what killed them. She asked lots of questions regarding our family and I thought you were the one who told her these. She asked why Prince had no wife at his age. **Me:** "ah you are now lying to me auntie Ha ha-ha... laughing No one has ever told Rosemary all that you have said. Rosemary lives in Masvingo so all stories about our village she knows nothing. "

Auntie: "You know Nigel your wife then she laid on the floor and started sniffing, twisting and turning like a snake eats poison. Within minutes, the whole floor was covered in water and i didn't even see where it was coming from. But the carpet which was at the door remained dry, it was awkward.

Your wife Nigel!! This incident left me speechless yesterday" She sighs... I tried to ignore the situation by going on the phone, she threw me water on the face, and then i left her and rumbled to my bedroom. When I arrived, there was water everywhere. Everything was wet except the bed only and that's why I called you to see for yourself." **Me:** "But I am not seeing any sign of water in the house and things you are saying is wet are dry. Why are you saying that aunt?" I asked this, but the issue of the water made me feels guilty because I have seen it too.

Auntie: "That's why I said come and get your person because it's so difficult for me. I don't know what to say, I wake up today want to take out wet things for them to get dry on the sun, but everything was not wet, without even a single drop of water on it. I went crazy for a second loitering the whole room searching for the wet clothes. Rosemary was standing at the door looking at me and asked me what I was looking for. I paused for a second, not knowing what to reply her. I asked her if she mopped that water which was on the floor. She puzzled and said she knew nothing about it. I tried to tell her what happened to her yesterday, but she made fun of me. Nigel your wife. "

Me: "Auntie probably you mistaken, or maybe hallucinating."

Aunty: "'Take your wife. You will see yourself my son. "

Then we got home and saw Rosemary bathing, singing religious songs. She finished, made our farewells to haunt the we hit the road she prepared us everything the bus rocked us from side to side as we traveled those familiar roads, our brains afforded the time to daydream or rest. There are those who chatter, their voices rising and blending together in the sweet ritual of friends. Some absorb themselves in music; others drift into worries that will erase themselves on arrival, when their body rejoins the world of moving and speaking to others. And so it goes on that way, all of us together and separate, feeling all the same turns and bumps.

It was an amazing journey back home. Past One pm we had arrived at Dombo, our village. We got home and Prince was absent. I asked Rosemary about what I had heard. She didn't answer then started crying and got out of the room and went to bed and cried there. I was left alone with stress all over my body. My thoughts became visible, they became an inverse explosion, crazy chaotic turns and twists of light all coming together to just one idea, to just one word. Another thought came of running away from Rosemary and go to Joburg where my other brother was staying. *Where i should say i was going?* I was planning this maths with my head facing down. When I raised my head I saw Rosemary standing at the bedroom door with her face angry, her eyes gleaming at me. I called her, "Hey love, come to daddy." she didn't come and said, "Nigel, why are you planning to leave me? You want to go to Johannesburg what i have done wrong to you?"

What!!!!!! *I was planning this now, how did she know about it?*

CHAPTER FOUR

I loved Rosemary with my whole heart. She was so nice to me and so elegant. I loved her seeing the last single beam of light from the sunset lighting up the surface of the endless ocean. She was like a painted masterpiece, with its greatness so absolute making the artist go mad with the realization of achieving nothing nearly as perfect. She was like love, the one and purely loves the kind of love that one would find themselves lucky to perceive only for a blink of an eye. Whenever she looked at me as I became inert, her beauty would strike in my bones; my mother told me that angels are in heaven, so what she was doing on earth. She stood still at the door peering at me with her dazzling bug eyed. Rosemary started to sob with the force of a person vomiting on all fours. It was hurtful to watch her like this; I felt my heart throbbed.

Then I stood up from where I was and moved to where she was standing then grabbed her and sat. All I could do was to embrace her and let the torrent of her tears to soak through my shirt. I could hear her silently screaming, suffocating with each breath she took onto her anger." I will never leave you Rosemary" I said running my fingers through her black long-hair, time and time again, in an attempt to calm the silent war within her mind. She looked at me like the fire in her eyes has been doused with ice water it makes the blue more pale. I'm not used to it, it unnerves me. I want her to give freely she always does but she won't. She just crawled right back inside this invisible shell and no matter how hard I try she's unreachable. She moves her eyes more slowly, like they're heavy, an effort to move. I want to crack my usual jokes, but I know she wasn't laughing. I'm standing right next to her but she might as well be on the moon. I blamed myself about the foolish plan of giving up on her. I told her what she had done at aunt's house in Harare, and further to tell me the truth about the watery stuff, but the child insisted that she was normal.

I ended up defending her that with her age she can't be responsible for doing these things. I am not sure why I was defending her without proper proof. Every thought of running away from her was over and I felt an extreme love for her and turned to love her so frequently. Rosemary kept on doing strange things... First day I missed her private things but the other day I saw it there. It was turning on and off like a sensor light. Some days i was left starving to death without having sex. This is what they call in love with a doll, whatever! That's the best way to describe it. Poor me. Mm, we began to love each other with Rosemary more than the first time. My relatives would come to see her and they would be thankful for the goodness and beauty of this child.

Even when we walked together, boys would be jealous and for sure I was feeling like a man and also a king. Everyone would stare at us and comment on how blessed I was to have this young angel in my life. The characteristics of being fish swimming in my dreams and doing mysterious things kept recurring. Telling her this about my dreams, she mocked me saying that I will become rich one day because fish it's a great sign of incoming wealth, a great fortune and a lot of money.

A lot of money? I wasn't believing in those fairy-tales since from my childhood age. Four months passed love being in the air. Falling in love with her was enjoyable and was like entering a house and finally realizing I'm home. When she smiles at me, I feel invisible hands wrapping around me, making me feel safe. When her eyes are locked on mine, it's like I can see galaxies instead of just pupils. Having her in my life makes me feel like everything's possible in this world, like I can conquer anything. But sometimes I regret meeting her and curse the day she came in my life. But there was no pregnancy. People started to laugh at me saying that I was infertile that's why I could not impregnate

Rosemary. *If it was Rosemary's side which have problem, how do they know?* You know, as a man failing to get someone pregnant is such an embarrassment. It troubled me big time until I came up with the idea of having another side chick secretly. *Let me try this advice and see it if I will fail.* I started dating a little girl lived in the north side of our village as i was staying south-side. I was no longer spending much time with Rosemary at home. This new girl was named Keith. I lied to Rosemary that I was going to play soccer daily, but Rosemary asked nothing. Some days she could ask what I was doing at North. I just thought maybe it was some gossip she had heard from someone who saw me there. I refused real objection to being in North that I was never been there.

I fell in love with Keith. Three months, Keith got pregnant. Lastly, lastly, I had silenced the devils by proving to them how wrong they were. I was the happiest man alive and was caught between heaven and earth for days. I spread this good news to every relative of mine and they told me to cast Rosemary out of the house because they need an heir. I came with a decision of taking Keith as my second wife, if Rosemary get hurt that's her problem, after all she was barren. One day I got out of bed early in the morning. Before the day started for the masses, I was already awake, fully dressed and ready to go. Outside it is as black as night, only by the clock can tell the difference between the time to sleep and the time to rise, to North to see my Keith and break the good news to her. I sneaked on Rosemary and jumped the fence yard so that she could not notice my way out. It was a distance. Within an hour, I was arrived at our meeting spot with Keith. I waited and waited, but no Keith was showing up. In this heat, I was barely formulated a thought.

There is no cooling breeze or cloud to block the high August sun. I curl my fingers around the thin fabric of my top, waving it in and out to create just a little air flow, but wasn't enough, like an ice cube into hot soup. Her last seen was showing yesterday at three p.m. A sudden onset of anger and frustration fell upon me and lay on the rock until I fell asleep and woke up around three without Keith coming. I was so angry, and I went back home with the frustration about Keith who disappointed me. I felt tightness in my chest Rosemary was already cooked supper. Once she saw me, she jumped out of joy and ran to hug and kissed me. This time I was not in the mood of this; what I needed was space. So isolated myself and i went to bedroom and began to think a lot. *Keith switched me her phone off, but she knows quite so well that we were supposed to meet and decided not to show up why? Maybe that pregnancy is not mine.* Hey, a sense of hatred towards Keith grew inside my black heart and swore by my parents' graves to never step my feet again there. Rosemary was so happy this day. All she was doing was making me feel more upset and worried about Keith. Prince came later that evening, and I left him playing with Rosemary. I was already inside the blankets. Even the moment Rosemary came to sleep, I did not hear a thing. I woke up the next morning, took my phone tried to reach Keith, but still was unavailable. Her voicemail kept uttering... sing your song after this beep... ahh this pissed me off again and again. "Where are you Kei?" I asked myself this question as if I was talking to a person who is listening. Rosemary was busy pulling me back in the blankets..." Daddy comes let's have some fun, I still want one last round of morning glory" Morning Glory was out of words, even to reply instead you will laugh. I was feeling bothered by her attention; I threw the blankets away from me and went outside the house. Sun was high in the sky and hot and plasma blue not evens a hand of cloud in the sky.

It was the best time to go to Keith's place. I went to Keith's house and saw his house packed with people scattered everywhere. It was my chance to get inside the yard. Keith's parents do not know about pregnancy only Keith. I came to realize that there was a tragedy at home or funeral. Then felt my heart clean and relieved. Now I know the reason why Keith's phone was off; she doesn't want to be distracted by phone calls whilst grieving. I sat where they were men hoping to see

Keith crossing by. An hour passed no Keith was coming. Then I asked a man I was sat next to, "who died here" He answered so confidently, "a young woman named Keith." Ha ha-ha... I laughed at him, this guy was so funny, maybe he knows me somehow wanted to play with my emotions. Then I got up and went to stay on the other side where they were children. Then asked a young boy to go inside the house and call Keith for me. Once found her, he should tell her that Daddy Nigel was around. "Keith died yesterday at the river"

He added without hesitation. I dragged him where there was no people and threatened him to tell me the truth not jokes. Me: "You said where Keith is?" Ah, Keith was caught yesterday by mermaids whilst washing clothes at the dam" "Where is the ladies she was with?" I asked confused. Then he showed me one of the women who was in the crowd and rushed there. She was the one who told me everything in detail the shocking news. Woman "Keith drowned at the dam yesterday to the side, which was not deep enough. At first we all thought she was playing with us but suddenly appeared a whirlwind from nowhere charging at us.

It chased us far from Keith isolating her alone. When it stopped, Keith was in the middle of the dam without even a slight chance of escaping. Her half body was exposed out of water like she was stepping on top of a rock so she was not struggling to keep her head up above the watery grave... We wanted to rescue her but something kept pushing her to the deepest side and the whirlwind was our greatest obstacle. Then came a huge monstrous fish, with its shimmering skin in the sunlight. We only saw its disgusting, deadly tail flickering out covering the whole Keith then pulled her inside the deep waters. When it disappeared, Keith was no longer to be found. Water swallowed them whole. People rushed home and explained this incident to the elders, and they said mermaids took her. Her mother heard that Keith had been taken away. She ran into the cold water and threw herself into the dam. Quite frankly, she was rescued by men and they called a Native doctor to help them to perform the ritual............

While in the middle of the ceremony, we saw Keith floating on top of water dead, at the exact same side her mother threw herself before. They took her body out of the water but were still warm showing signs that moments ago she was still alive. And that mermaid.....” She didn't finish explaining, and another woman called her to help prepare food. I couldn't hold myself after hearing this shocking news; my mind went blank for a second. I went inside where there were rows of chairs, with a front row of fancier chairs for the immediate family. In front of the chair is an open space, and then the casket was displayed and fell down there. Keith was no more with my baby. Once the first tear broke free, the rest followed in an unbroken stream. I bent forward on the floor pressing my palms to the mat sobbing so hard. People hold me, comforting but her relatives and parents shocked a lot about who I was and why I was crying so hard than others, they don't know me, not even a relative. Whilst grieving, Rosemary called. Me: “he he, hello... Ba. b. b... a. baby. I am busy right now, I will call you soon” then I cut the call. I tried to explain to people maybe if they could call an ambulance she would have change to survive as her body was still warm. No one minded me and I tried to call the ambulance myself but they were no network coverage. In the middle of struggling to search the network, Rosemary called again.

I picked up the phone and answered with an angry voice. “I said I will call you Rosemary” Hello, Rosemary, I'm busy i will call you soon.”

CHAPTER FIVE

"Rosemary please, I told you to..." I was trying to control my tears and my voice but she recognized that I was grieving and started laughing at me. "Why are you crying, babe? Are you okay, Nigel?" This disturbed me and more anger and annoyance was inflamed and hanged up the call. I was just a man who just lost everything. I mean everything I ever cared about. *Why Keith, why you die with my child?* I felt my emotions tapping outside of my mind as I began unleashing my hatred towards the mermaid that killed her, Stream of liquid started trickling down my face could cure my pain. All this was like the manifestation of a real dream even though I tried to wake up by slapping my miserable face time and time again, but I wasn't walking up. Until I saw her casket being carried away to the burial ground, that's when I realized it wasn't a dream anymore. When the coffin was being lowered to the ground, many tears were shed, paying their respect to Keith for the untempt time... it was a thorny in the flesh and I was hurt, Keith left me with everlasting unbearable anxiety.

The wound that no one can heal. When the funeral was over, I was left behind alone at the cemetery owing my last goodbyes to the mother of unborn child. On my way back home, I was not being myself, moving in a zigzag way, staggering like a drunkard bustard that was under the influence of alcohol. I wiped my watery tears at the door before entering the house and disguised as if everything was fine. Rosemary was on her happy mode as usual. She was sitting on the couch waiting for my arrival. She came and gave me a greeting both a missing kiss and a warm hug. "Good evening, Daddy, I missed you my love. Food is ready and how was your day been?" running her soft fingers through my bearded chin which was growing. "I am fine Rosemary." Her attention was disturbing me. I gradually distanced myself from her by isolating myself in the bedroom. What I was only needed was space, to be alone, then I started sobbing very hard with my hand covered the whole mouth that no sound of crying should come out... After Keith's passing, the mourning had not run its course.

The heaviness was in my limbs as much as my mind. Things she used to find funny now only caused a deepening of the pain. Rosemary followed me with food on the tray and remained at the door. "Daddy, Daddy, Daddy, are you sure you are ok?" she said putting the tray on the bed, a dimple appeared at the corner of her mouth. Quickly, I wiped my tears so quick; she lifted her head and gazed at me in the eyes and saw that I was crying. She gave me my plate full of food but I refused to eat, then she started eating. "Nigel I'm sorry, I didn't mean to .... ah sorry mmm I mean why are crying? What happened? She snorted. "I am not crying, you didn't mean what?" I asked her turning my body facing the other side of the bed, as a sign of ignoring. "I'm sorry about the baby, Keith; I don't mean to .... ki. L... I mean I didn't know that you were having another wife" putting a hunk of meat inside her mouth.. "Nigel, tell me something, right? Am I not beautiful as other girls?"

What other women has I don't have? Or you do not love me anymore, which made you to choose that bloody bitch over me? You are still playing boy> you don't know me very well" she added devouring her meat. "Rosemary, what are you trying to say?" Now she got my attention. She is threatening me who she really thinks she is? A moment of silence broke for about a minute, with many questions in my mind as if I was trying to solve simultaneous equations inside my head. Whatever can silence be? For is there not always the sound of your own heart? Just as with whiteness there is light, and blackness is a canvass for dreams; if there is a soul present, there is always something. And so as the quietness grows deeper, and I heard my own steady rhythm from within, I call this silence. *So it means Rosemary now knows my secrets about my affair with Keith? What she was trying to say when saying I am still playing? Who told her about Keith's death and the pregnancy? This girl argh........* I saw it was better to swallow my pride and persuaded her in a polite way so that she can tell me everything she knows. "Babe who told you about Keith?

Rosemary: "Keith was my friend, she told me everything about your affair and your plans" What!!! It can't be she laying... let me end the conversation, she will tell me her story tomorrow, today I have so many fish to fry. "I had enough of your lies and accusation. I am sleeping." I faced the wall again and slept. Once fallen asleep, here goes again my water dream, but this time I wasn't swimming, I was sitting outside the dam. Rosemary was the one who kept diving inside the dam over and over again. Then came to check me how I was doing then dove back again. The following morning, I awake to the steady patter of rain upon my window, droplets yet to scatter the nascent rays of the rising sun. The sound brings calmness to mind, a soothing melody, and a natural lullaby. With eyes at rest I feel my center, live happily within myself for these blessed moments of solitude. I found me and myself alone in the blankets. I tossed the blankets off me and went to check outside. She was packing clothes inside a dish. One thing I favored about Rosemary, no matter how much we fight or quarrels, her love doesn't change. She will treat you with respect and perfect love you think you deserve. "Morning daddy how was your night?" she said with a pleasant smile and a dimple comes out at the corner of her mouth.

That love sensation fell upon me quickly and ran and hugged her. Unfortunately, everything I wanted to ask her was forgotten, I don't know why, maybe that's what love does every time. ." Daddy please accompany me to the dam to wash clothes. Here it's quite boring and another thing, I want to see new places please Daddy" she asked going inside the house to take pegs and washing powder. The dam she was talking about was the very same dam where Keith was killed. She got courage indeed, or maybe she doesn't know the dam she was talking about. "No, I won't take you to that dam or allow you to go there. There are mermaids, if they take you what would I do?" truly, that dam was deadly and I can't afford to lose them both. Rosemary was the only one left, so I should do everything in my power to protect her. Quite amazing, she started laughing and teasing me, "Daddy you are chicken-hearted, you get scared so easily like a woman. You are afraid of mermaid's things you don't even know if they exist or not? Come on love, let's go nothing will happen," she said, bravely carrying her dish on top of her head and started heading forth.

"Wait Rosemary, I said you are not going anyway I mean it" I was trying to stop the one and only person I ever cared about. With all these weird stories, I heard about the mysteries of this dam. And a glimpse of what I had heard about Keith's capture, hell no we can't go. "No, Daddy we are going" she stared at me so hard with a bewitching eye vigorously without blinking. Next I don't know what happened. I only find myself, rushing inside the house, collected my towel and start following her to the dam. We arrived at this devil's dam, quite scary and weird to look. The darkness and fog made it hard for me to see the end of the sidewalk. There were no people around the dam was the dam that drowned my Keith. No one was at the dam and they was another side of this dam which was having no water but mud only and long green grass and reeds. No one goes there even animals because they will be stuck in this muddy place... As I was the one on front leading the way, I went to the side where people used to wash and bath themselves. People were afraid to come here because of the incident that had happened here to Keith. **Rosemary** 'babe I don't want to wash clothes here." she refused to put her dish down. **Me** "So where because this is the only place people wash their clothes" She remained quiet and started going forth to the side where they were quick mud... "Rosemary, come back that side is dangerous. Okay goodbye I am going back home" I said this, warning her and started going back facing home direction. My gut was twisting once arrived at this dam. *What if the mermaid comes? It could be our end.* I hid behind a certain rock trying to scare Rosemary. Once she looks back and find me no more, what could be her reaction? That's what I wanted to see. Indeed, she took a few steps then looked back and saw.

BANG!! This was a sound of her dish being dropped to the ground followed by a loud scream... "Daddy, daddy, daddy, help, mermaid, help!"

This is the moment you will see the entire world spinning and closing in. I was paused, my body was frozen, and the shock had wrapped my body. I tried to move a muscle but was paralyzed by shock and fear. All I could hear was my pulse thudding in my ears. Another though was saying, *run Nigel runaway with your life. But what about my wife? I should go on and save her, but I told her not to come here in the first place. Now what?* I was mixed up not knowing what to do. I never prayed in my life that was my first time praying to God. They is this say, **when people are in trouble, it is the time they know the existence of God.** I went on my knees and prayed a silent prayer with my eyes and ears wide open being aware of my surroundings. With my heart pounding very quickly. Panic was rising like bile in my system. This dam was located at the remote areas outskirts to the village, so if you scream no one will hear you. To make matters worse, the story of Keith's death injected fear to people finished my short prayer then started crawling forth towards where I heard Rosemary screaming. Only her dish was on the ground with clothes scattered everywhere as a witness to her disappearance. This injected more fear and shock in my body, which made me walk backwards step by step. Water in the dam was steady and silent as if nothing had happened not even a sound. Whilst still wondering and overwhelmed by this hair-raising moment, a sound of a stone thrown by a person in the dam heard. Quickly, I looked back to that side and was no one. Tendrils of terror curried into my stomach.

My back was now facing the dam, and I felt a puff of breath at the back of my neck, something invisible which was cold wrapping my neck like a snake. A splash of more fear hit me as I touched back to check what it was but was nothing, my fingers were pinching straight to my very own skin. You know how difficult it is to fight the invisible force or to run. You will run to where it is launched. *Nigel! You're crazy. You are afraid of something you have never seen.* Another thought was telling me to be brave and steady. But the other was telling me to run whilst there is still time, or else end was near. Whilst moving backwards, I stepped on something and fell inside the dam... poor Nigel. At first, water flooded in, my throat burned as if thousands needles had been plunged into it. The exit was very near and started to swim very fast longing to escape. I was aware on my legs, making sure nothing was touching my legs. A sudden wind started from nowhere raging at me and started dragging me to the deepest side of the dam. You can't oppose the wind and win the battle. Every time I was near exist, it kept pushing me back in the middle of the dam.

I tried more and more to oppose it by pushing with my arms and legs but could not find leverage. It kept dragging me to the center of the death ring again and again. Seeing that this is the end, I screamed a loud scream which echoes the mountains nearby and scares the whole birds of the forest and they flew away with terror. It was a foolish move because no one will hear me, but was another contribution to my exhaustion. Luckily, I reached a small rock which was in the middle of the dam and sat on top of it.

It was my lifesaver, more than an hour struggling, fighting for my survival. What surprised me is, my head was dry never become wet, all the time I thought of drowning myself, I found myself floating on top of the water. I recalled all my previous dreams swimming in the dam and knew its interpretations. My dreams were telling me about this moment. Ha ha-ha I heard laughter coming from where I started drowning. It was a high cold cackle, piercing the smoky air. Voices of women giggling and kept drawing closer and closer. Two seconds passed by and saw it was Rosemary coming alone.

Who was she talking to? Me; Rosemary, run home and call the people to come and get me out of this place when still talking, she took a dove like a dolphin and remained underwater for minutes, how was she breathing?

CHAPTER SIX

I saw Rosemary coming out from the dam where she spent approximately three minutes without breathing, coming to me with a hug. "Daddy, what happened? Huh Nigel, how did you reach here?" she asked being agitated; Also, Rosemary expressed worry about how I come to that place at the center of the deadly dam. The cold moved in only to meet the warmth of my blood, though I was on the sun, my defense against such cold water was washed over my skin, again and overly, merely to be contacted by the beat of my heart, again and again. I couldn't even talk because of the coldness, which was still in my body. All the time I spent swimming caused my muscle to froze. Rosemary was acting so mysterious at the dam. *Where she was all the time? I heard her falling in the water. Who was she laughing too?*

Many questions filled in my mind. Now it was all made clear to me that Rosemary was not that kind of girl to fall in love with. "Hold on Daddy, it's time to leave" she said carrying me on her tiny back and began swimming heading to exist. We reached outside, and I laid on another small rock. Rosemary took dry clothes from the dish and tossed them to me to change. All the fear was vanished, I was having this gut sense that the owners of this place are around nothing bad will happen to me. Rosemary puzzled me because her clothes she was wearing when she came to rescue me was dry not even a single drop of water in it. How? She was swimming with them. She started washing few clothes, my eyes gleaming on her with a withering glare. **Rosemary:** "Daddy lets wash clothes that side where there is reeds, fragrance cosmetics is not allowed here? "Who told you that soap is not allowed?" I asked with an angry voice. "I know Nigel, mermaid don't like fragrance cosmetics things. That's why Keith was captured and killed," she answered confidently, holding me with my hand so that we could move from that place.

I was still exhausted and my head was arching, my eyes burning and my legs had given up. There's a kind of tired that needs a good night's sleep, and another that needs so much more. For me, one became the other, starting out as the "one night kind" until one day it was ever present - like it once was a heavy jacket but became heavy bones. It was that being tired was being a wearing of the emotions too, that can come together with a tired body, and become an ingrained part of a life that isn't lived, but survived, endured I refused to go. "Go by yourself you will find me here sleeping."

Rosemary: "Why are you stop stubborn Nigel? Could you stop bickering for a second, please? If you stay here, they will come and take you again and put you back inside the dam as before" then she started going forth to the side where there was long grass and mud. **Me'hey** you Rosemary! Come back now and tell me who will to take me back inside the dam?" indeed this girl was so weird who are they that will put me in water? I felt fear shuttering my bones and stood up then started following her. I wiped the sweat from my brow with a trembling hand, fear from my narrow escape coursing through my veins. She went exactly to the side where people couldn't reach and started advancing inside the long grass and reeds. "Babe, where are you going? That side there is no water but mud only, you will sink there. Let's go home, please." I was trying to persuade her, but she kept on advancing, ignoring my warning. She stopped at a place where there was a small tree surrounded by reeds and green grasses, then putted her dish down. We're been far away from water now. "Rosemary tell me something. How are you going to wash here because they are no water?"

Rosemary "That's why you are here my beautiful husband. you are the one who will fetch me water from the dam. " What!!!!!!!!!!!!! No matter how hard I deny, with her single stare, I will turn to do whatever she asks. Describe a strange tree I sat under this tree, started observing my surroundings, which was scary and promising danger. It was like a haunted place with whispering ghosts. "Not here again Nigel, let's keep going" she said heading forth deeper and deeper inside this disgusting long grass until she was invisible. At first I was wondering if maybe she was playing mind games with me, wanted to see my reaction. I stood up and threw a stick to where she was going to scare her but she doesn't look scared or shaken at all. I threw for the second time a big stone, but she kept ignoring. **Me** " Rosemary, so you come here to kill me right? You know that since morning we have put nothing in our stomachs. I am starving to death. " "Wait Daddy I am coming now, darling. Are you sure you want to leave your wife here alone?" My stomach growled, and I squirmed on where I was sat to silence the rumbling. I glanced at the clock; it was almost lunchtime. My eyes glazed over as I imagined the sandwich in my bag next to my feet. I was salivating at the thought of it. Only one more minute. I was starving until fallen asleep. I woke up around two and was still alone. "Rosemary, what are you still doing you are now scaring me? You don't even finished washing yet."

Rosemary: "Daddy, Daddy, come here and see this! Run?" Quickly, I stood up and rushed to where she was inside the reeds. Wow!!!!!! That place she was was amazing and enjoyable to look. They was a small spring with shining sand and a small cave with small silver fish hovering inside. This place seemed it always cleaned and swept all the time. Its waters was Mediterranean-blue and magical.

It was swishing over the rocks joyfully. It was thundering down into the dam like a gigantic water spout. When it toppled into the ecstasy-pool, it foamed it at the bottom. The rest of the pool was as clear as cellophane, enabling us to see down into the rocky bottom. Fronds of forest-green plants waved gently in the depths. Its edges were hemmed with whipped-white lines. We could see a gaggle of geese grazing by the bank and the scene was picture perfect. A group of Amazonian ferns, edged with saw's teeth and statue still, added a tropical flavor. It gave me goose bumps immediately. The nectar sweet smell of the spring flowers perked up our spirits with its honey sweet smell. This place was like a paradise on earth and I wanted to spend my entire life here. I kept looking at this place. Rosemary was the one who dragged me to go. We arrived back where we left our clothes before. Surprisingly, was already washed and hung on thorny bushes to dry up. Only few was left. Instead of being surprised or asking Rosemary who washed our clothes?

Nope. I rushed to check them, touching if they were still wet as if I had an idea who put them there. Rosemary was looking at me with her smile on her face like she is watching a baby making first steps. "Nigel, let's fetch some water so we can finish these clothes which is left?" "Okay my love," I replied, taking the dish. I carried the dish and started racing each other to where water was laughing at each other, as what we always do when everything is in order. We didn't take food with us but amazingly; I saw Rosemary giving me a small basket full of roasted fish. Without asking again, we started devouring our food happily. All the terror of being terrorized was gone, and I was in my own world of love. It was like Romeo and Juliet's movie. She started washing clothes, and I sneaked her and went to that amazing place where they was having a small curve and silver less water in color.

This time I was alone without being disturbed by Rosemary and then sat on a small rock so I could be able to see the whole view. The sense of getting back home was already left in me because this place made me forget everything even my bundle of misery was flashed out. The opposite side of the small curve were fragrance flowers which were perfumed, fragrant, scented, sweet smelling, pungent, usually pleasing - it is not odorless and unscented. Actually, I had no idea how long I spent on this place gazing on this small curve. Strange laughter which was coming to where Rosemary was distracted me who is she laughing too again? Now I will find out myself I rumbled there without making strange sounds so I should not disturb them. No one was there only Rosemary. But clothes were added on the line, which were not belongs to us. Instead of asking her, I started playing with her over and over again. Then I left her and went to my beautiful spot. I heard this strange sound of a big object like a hippopotamus threw itself in water. Quite disturbing, I stood up trying to have a look but was nothing. I went to check on Rosemary for the third time. On my arrival, I saw rids and grass surrounds that area of the dam shaking.

Another splash of terror struck me and as I was about to run, a hand touched me at my shoulder, "Daddy, what are you afraid of?" said Rosemary removing her cold her off my shoulder.

Ha ha ha ha..... The laugh continues

"I never see a man who acts like a woman like you, never." **Me:** "Rosemary, let's go now. I have heard something in water. Maybe it's a mermaid" I was dragging her by her hand although she was refusing to leave. I was frustrated and swallowed that anger when it was a fire-seed and forgot to drink something cool, and so it grew in my belly until it came out as hot as any dragon has ever flamed. **Me:** "But babe tell me, where did you come from when you touch my shoulder that side they is no way but only water?" I was quite disturbed because they was no road or ground but only water. "Stop asking this grade zero questions, Nigel. Let's go home before sun fall, time is not our side. You always talk about mermaids did you saw them before?" "No. I only heard people talking about them and how dangerous they are," I replied. "Do you want me to show you Daddy?"

This girl is crazy indeed. She thinks she can show me mermaids. Where? This made me laugh with my stomach. I was at the opposite side of her; her right hand was inside water playing with it. So she came to me with water inside her palm and splashed me very hard on the face. It was painful and poor boy, as I was trying to rub my eyes, something which reflected as a silver light in the water which mirrored in the almost unruffled eyes and where a ripple curled it the tiny crest glittered like white flame and that harmed my vision by damaging the eye's retina, "It covered the whole place this silver reflection, and I remembered myself falling inside the dam.

Me: "Rosemary, I am your husband, please"………

CHAPTER SEVEN

I didn't see her again because of the reflection causing my eyes to rest upon golden arcing rays, illumination that gives vivacious hues to this underwater world. I felt sinking in the water, struggling to breathe but was feeling pain or water feeling water soaking in my lungs. Amazingly. I was like moving without using my legs like, maybe flying. It was as if my body was being transformed into an astral body... Type of this nature I felt so thrilled; I was traveling with the momentum of a thought. Any place I felt like going within moments I was there underwater. I was being in another world, where you can't touch the ground but manifesting and creating anything with your mind. I began to think of Rosemary, Prince, and Keith. Where were there? Already forgotten than Keith had died? I began to explore the area having that alone feeling? They spoke, once you have mastered being alone; you are ready for the company of others, that doesn't make it easy though. When everyone's life journey separated from my own, when the only heart beating on this very dam belonged to me, it wasn't something most could take. It is the time when the brain becomes a cold fire, perhaps that is what others call panic.

As I was fluttering around hoping to find people there in front of my way placed a basket full of roasted fish. Though I was starving, I decided not to eat any of those because it's stealing. I don't even know the owner or who leave it there. I kept on moving forth and in front of me was a place which was covered in darkness. It was like the world has become a pencil drawing, a masterpiece on the easel of the creator. I wait for it to fade to black and arise anew. It is as if the nightfall were the curtains closing. Even to wave your hand in front of you, the visibility would be zero. How tangible this darkness was, so spooky. I started to move backwards where they was light and seemed safer. **Ha.ha.ha......** The same laughter I heard before but now Rosemary's voice was in it couple of distance withdrawn about a stone's throw, a mile away, it would echo through the walls of the dam and into every ear. It was a laughter that you could feel in your lungs, so hard that it nearly took my breath away. The lack of oxygen didn't matter. All the anguish of struggling to find people melted like snowballs in a microwave. But they were invisible. I rushed where the voices were coming but kept going far from me. The moment I was getting closer, that's how far the voices go. Is it ghost voices or what, why are they unreachable? I said to myself trying to figure out, but I was hearing Rosemary's voice. Frustration grew in me; Finally, I decided not to follow these voices and started moving the opposite where.

They placed the same very bucket of roasted fish on my path, this time I had wasted no time. I feast myself, two minutes the bucket was empty. Those fish was so nice and taste. I wandered the owner who cooked it deserves a trophy. Strange voices kept laughing and talking but it seemed as if they were talking about me. "Rosemary, Rosemary, Rosemary, I know it's you" I called out her name with a loud voice. I started to be myself bit by bit. I remembered how a mermaid attacked and killed Keith and how I fall inside the dam because of Rosemary who splashed me water to my face. *So Rosemary was the one who brought me here, right? And now her voice is talking here; indeed, she has something to do with all this. Where I am right now? What is this place?* Many questions flooded inside my mind without answers. I heard gospel songs being sung inside my head and I prayed but no change came. "Lord, show me where I am, please. I am begging you" My body was now exhausted of floating; I tried and failed to sit down because of a zero gravity place, no ups and downs. Moments later, fish started appearing and sounds of birds in a distance by. I felt a little bit relieved and comfortable because now this place was promising life. The same direction where fish came from comes Rosemary swimming surrounded by many fishes. Suddenly; all of them came and made a circle around me. Also Rosemary came and held my hand, saying nothing.

"But why Rosemary, why?" Tears broke out uncontrollably but she looked not caring at all. There was a side she wanted us to go, "no babe please Rosemary don't do that to me" She remained silent as if she was deaf. She spoke with signals to the fish, then they all came behind me and saw myself moving going towards the direction where Rosemary was going. That side the atmosphere was different, they was misty, and real color of the earth started to manifest in effect a successive shifting of zones of vegetation. Only the silver reflection was the only left obscuring my eyes until I could hardly see that I was already outside lying on my back on top of the rock. But I was naked only wearing my underwear only. I stood to check what happened and saw Rosemary at the opposite side playing with water. I was still recalling everything inside my head. I went to put on my clothes and check the time and see, 06:43 am. *What?????* We had left home at 8:40 pm. I looked at the date was telling me that we were here yesterday. *How?* Anybody who can explain this... *So where did we slept yesterday?* I asked myself and fought hard trying to figure out what happened, but I started to lose memory right away. I forgot everything and started asking myself *where my wife is?* I rushed to her and carried her up on my hands going to where our clothes was. What puzzled me is that our clothes were already packed nicely inside the dish. Rosemary wandered too about this incident. Her face fell faster than a corpse in cement boots. In that instant her skin became greyed.

Her mouth hung with lips slightly parted and her eyes were as wide as they could stretch. **Rosemary**: "Tell me what is going on? Where do you sleep Nigel; leaving your wife alone the whole night?" she started crying heavily on my shoulders. For sure I blamed myself for leaving her alone though I tried very hard to remember where exactly I slept, but no answer was coming? "Nigel, are you serious to leave me alone in this jungle alone where they are monsters? If I got taken by mermaids, what could you do? Happy right?" I remained silent assuming what was wrong with me. Lastly, I put the blame on my sister who was in U. K that maybe she is the one behind all this, or maybe she was using me to get rich. I felt hatred rising towards my sister. Hate colored the soul and spreads throughout the entire system, shutting down all other feelings, and becoming central to life. *I want to go home, buy airtime and expose her.* "Sorry my love to put you in this situation. I will tell you all you should know at home. I am really sorry Rosemary, please forgive me. It will be fine let's go home now. I know what is happening my love," I said, rubbing her back with my hand and started moving. "You know what is going on?" she asked me looking surprised and stopped sobbing immediately. "Yes love. But never mind about it. I will tell you everything" I added with anger and hatred burning inside me.

I wasn't a hero until you came I knew what she was doing to me. Then it will be war. She crossed the line and I don't forget. I won't rest until I expose her and I don't mean just exposed only. I mean her devilish heart gets rid of. Now she can't hide, I will find her, and then destroy her. I don't much care how it happens; I don't need her to suffer. I just need her cold black eyes extinguished from this universe. This is not an overreaction, but it is the truth. Really, my own sister went to U. K London to use me so that she can be prosperous and what did I get in return... nothing only these fucking weird moments? She will see me. We went back home and saw Prince at home being stressed and frustrated about our whereabouts and where we slept yesterday. He started yelling at us as if we were young children. "Where are you coming from now since yesterday? Where the hell have you been and where did you sleep last night? Nigel, you think you are now old enough to do whatever pleases you? You want me to get into trouble with your sister Patricia?" He started clenching his fist too hard, and gritted teeth from effort to remain silent; his hunched form exuded an animosity that was like acid - burning, slicing, and potent. His face was red with suppressed rage, I never saw Prince been so angry like this. He showed me the dark side of himself. It seemed he didn't sleep the whole night being worried about his younger brother. **Prince:** "I am waiting for an answer, Nigel."

I remained silent and went inside the house, avoiding being beaten, walking past him whilst talking. Prince was waiting for an answer outside with Rosemary. "And you Rosemary, where the hell have you been with Nigel? Doing what?" "Ask your young brother he knows everything" she replied pointing fingers at me. When I heard Rosemary being troubled by Prince, my anger and frustration was aroused to the extent of failing to control myself and rushed again outside, you are asking us as if you don't know what is going on really Prince? Why did you not tell me all along? Prince? Why didn't you tell me? Wait for me I am coming back. " My voice was uproarious, very loud and noisy, which was on top of his. That's scared the hell out of him and remained silent. Even our neighbors this day heard me yelling at Prince. I saw Rosemary smiling. Quickly, I came with my airtime and recharged my phone on my way back home. That vision of me underwater was still recalling. I felt sorry for Rosemary, why they are troubling her? *She was the one who saved me from drowning. But why didn't she tell me what happened? Only God knows.* I went inside the house and sat on the couch with sweat covering my whole body. There's a certain level of tiredness that equates to insanity; for me it's when I'd like to temporarily dislocate my spirit from my body, as if I could ask God to take me out for just a short while, let my soul go wherever souls goes. I started calling Patricia. Prince and Rosemary followed in the house with all ears. **Me:** Hello, hello!!!! **Patricia:** "My lovely brother Nigel, hello my sweet brother," she answered with a sweet, loving, caring voice.

Me:

Chapter Eight

Me: Really, Patricia? You are making too much money because of me. Right?" **Patricia:** "What are you saying, baby boy. I miss you my little brother. What do you want me to bring you from London?" **Me:** "So you are seeing me as your rightful candidate to use your charms on, so that you will become rich?" **Patricia:** "What? You sound serious indeed Nigel. Who is using Muti (charms) against whom? Me!!!!!!! Okay brother, I will be there next week on Monday then you will tell me that crazy story of yours" she hung the call, seemed angry and puzzled about my allegations. These strong accusations require sustained mental attention that will benefit to refresh my mind was distracted, by having a walk to stretch my legs and clear my head. I went outside the house to refresh with these thoughts.

When our parents died, Patricia was the one who took care of me and paid all my school fees. Even from clothing, I was a step ahead with style compared to other to other boys in the village because of Patricia. Everything I ever wanted she gave me, how she would do that to me? If she comes and kicks me out of the house where did I go? Maybe my conjectures are incorrect? What if I told her what is happening maybe she could help me? At the moment, that flash of frustration protected me from the pain. Where I to relive it, I would try to summon more strength. "Everything will be okay Daddy, don't stress right" said Rosemary touching my shoulder and sat next to me with her arm around my waist. I slowly and length nodded my head showing agreement and understanding, but was just disguising her to believe that I was on the same page.

Rosemary: "Nigel, I love you my husband. I don't know how to thank God for giving me a good-hearted husband like you. Be the man, put stress on God.... hmmm our god helps us Daddy. I am here for you" she added with her hand running over my chest. **Me**: "I love you too, Rosemary, thank you for saving my life yesterday. I didn't know that you are a good swimmer" for sure she deserves my compliment, without her I don't know. Oh... Nigel guys, so you're telling me that you were failing to get out of that dam? I was watching you waiting to see if you could escape."

She added with a very slow sweet voice. "You did a great job out there. I thought I was dying. Where did you learn to swim?" **Rosemary**: "Where I came from they call me a sea-diver. I once saved two girls who were captured by mermaids. Unfortunately, one died the other survived. People who were there said I was the one who killed her. That my retribution I get from them." **Me**: "They said you killed her how? Tell me about it, love. " **Rosemary**: "you know, Nigel. It's a long story, but let me tell you in short. I was just coming from school and I saw a crowd gathered on the river. They told me what happened to the girls. So I told them not to cry I should try to get inside the dam and get them out... They thought I was bluffing at first until they saw me undressing and took a dove inside. Daddy, I took time underwater searching for the girls. I saw one girl still alive, you know I had to run away, but I was just too brave and

I went to where she was with the mermaids, grabbed her and started swimming out of the dam. We arrived at the surface and show people the girl. No one seemed happy or crying Daddy. **Me**: "Why?" **Rosemary**: "If they cry, the girl should die. So they took her, and I dove back again to search for the last one" **Me**: "So, baby, how where you breathing underneath? Were you not getting exhausted for swimming that long? Why those mermaids did didn't attack you? You said if they cry the girl dies, how because you were already out of the dam with her?" **Rosemary**: "Why so many questions? Which one to answer now? It's better not to continue the story," she replied, showing being distracted by my questions. I persuaded her to continue. "Sorry Rosemary, it's only that I am eager to know the whole story. Sorry you may continue to love. " **Rosemary:** "I started swimming down, deeper and deeper showing courage. I saw her still alive again surrounded by a group of mermaids. I took her and the mermaids did nothing, but to stare at me going with their prey. At first, I thought maybe they will follow me behind but they didn't daddy. When I was on top of the watery grave, I showed again people the second girl. Her mother jumped out of joy and tears of joy overflowed on her cheeks and this upsets one of the mermaids. She followed me Daddy and you know what? People saw it live because it came and exposed half of its human body out of the water. And sunken its 4inches-nails directly to the girl's neck and blood followed oozing out coloring the whole dam. Instantly it disappeared Nigel. So I went outside with the body and people began to say I was the one who killed the girl, but they all saw what happened. People are always people Daddy, instead of thanking me for my effort that's the reward I got from them. They dismissed themselves and they left me alone at this river.

You know what I saw Daddy?" **Me** "What did you see Rosemary?" I was quite shocked about what Rosemary was telling me. **Rosemary** 'It was too much, Nigel. I saw men with reeds plunged on their backs, Fresh green reeds, coming out of the dam to the shore. A person who will see them assumes that's it was only reeds of the dam then step on top of them. They came a little gazelle want to drink water then stepped on top of this people. Within a couple of seconds, I saw the gazelle being floating on top of the dam, these people they sank underneath and started to drag this poor animal underneath the dam. It's too much daddy I can't finish." she stood up and held my hand and we went inside the house. I was speechless. We arrived in the bedroom and she came and lay on top of my chest. "Daddy, you know, mermaids are so cruel? They had no remorse, if they take a person without relatives or with dead parents, they make that person to grow reeds on his/her back" I just nodded my head but I was totally shocked about all these mysteries she was telling me.

Rosemary: "When we grew up, they told us this entire daddy. Now people were calling me little mermaid because I know too much. " Ha ha-ha... she started giggling, "Others were saying all the time I spent underwater, I changed into a mermaid, but I saw nothing Daddy." If she lies, you will believe her because she had that talking mentality and a good take. If she is around, you don't need any entertainment media because she always keeps talking until you are tired of listening to her. Sometimes I wonder from where she gets the huge energy for speaking. She was loved by all of our family members and even in the neighborhood. But people were not knowing her other dark version of herself. I don't know what she was trying to mean by telling me all these and at the end she will say she was normal. I suspected her that truly she was having something to do about Keith's death. Even my fall in the dam and spending the whole night underneath, she was behind all those incidents. I saw it was better to go to her parents and tell them what was happening to their child. **Me** "Tomorrow, I will see your parents and ask them what is wrong with you. You are scaring me now Rosemary. I mean now not tomorrow. " She tried to stop me and saw me putting on my shoes. **Rosemary**: "Please, Nigel don't do that. Where do you think you are going?"………

CHAPTER NINE

Rosemary told me an exceedingly complex story here. I saw it was better for me to see her sister. She looked at me tying my thread, and rushed to Prince's room and woke him up. "Daddy Prince come and see what your brother is doing here. He is going to my parents' house without even paid the dowry or even a single cow. What does it mean? You know it is against our tradition. Please wake up and stop him," she said, being afraid of me going to their parents. I don't know what she was avoiding me to go. They came out together with Prince and tried to stop me, but my ignoring was so loud that was deafening. This silence was so deep that was echoing I was the one possessing power now to do whatever I want. As I was walking followed by Rosemary and Prince, couple of steps then stopped abruptly. I saw them glaring at me hardly doing nothing. I started to ask myself *what I was going to do. When I got to her sister, what I will say I am here for?*

I started to feel sorry for Rosemary and blamed myself for being abusive. *Maybe I should listen to my wife and listen to whatever she asserts.* I was distracted from my opinions by a deadly heavy wind which emerged from nowhere, pursued by a gigantic storm. The bone-chilling cold seemed unbearable in the howling wind. The sound of thunder rolled through the area as another lightning bolt split the sky. **Rosemary:** "Daddy run, be careful of that storm impending, run back here." Immediately I spun my back and started pacing and took Rosemary and raced inside the house. The rain pattered the rooftop. I looked out the window, the sky was tar-black and the large clouds were moving fast. When my first foot stepped inside the bedroom, the loving sensation continues and turned to embrace her more. Days and weeks passed in love with my wife Rosemary. Everything was going well. We organized money for her dowry and went to pay half of it, but they refused the money. They suggested us to take her for free. *They refused our money, why? Aren't the one who delivered her clothes to us? So what's the problem?* I realized that on these issues I was young. *Now I want to hold a grudge with my sister.*

Days passed by, and Patricia came from U.K. London. I told her everything, what was happening to my life since Rosemary involved in my life. As an adult, she felt that for sure something wasn't right on Rosemary. We arranged to visit her sister. That day arrived, and we told Rosemary exactly where we were going. **Rosemary:** "Nigel, don't start things you cannot finish with your sister, you will regret soon.

I told you to go once when they received the dowry. But your heads are so stubborn. " "No babe, we will not see other relatives but your sister only. I am going with Patricia to see her so that they could know each other better. Bye see you when we are back" I said these calming words giving her a goodbye kiss on the cheek. This day, the weather was so clear with no cloud cover. Amazingly with no further due, it changed abruptly. Large pillows of clouds started forming followed by large drops of rain. We made a U-turn sprinting white ice balls hitting our heads hardly. We arrived back home being wet, and I rushed to the bedroom to change. Rosemary laughed at me that we failed to go. We changed the day to the next day when the weather was cleared. The following day we tried to go but rain stopped us again. Every time we was about to go, rain started from nowhere and stopped us. Rosemary swore and bet with me that no matter what circumstances I will never see her sister. This made Patricia to hate Rosemary with all her guts. She told me that Rosemary was a mermaid or had something to do with mermaids. Although we planned to go to her parents to tell us the truth, all our plans failed because rain always stopped us. One day we went out with Patricia with her car to town only two of us because

Patricia and Rosemary were holding a grudge against each other, plus blood is thicker than water as you know. Lucky, we associated with Rosemary's sister at the supermarket.

She was happy to meet with us and was eager to see me all along, but she said rain always stopped her also. We greeted each other and sat in the car and started our peaceful conversation. **Patricia:** "We wanted to pay the dowry to your house." **Rosemary's sister**: "Ooh!!!! That's a good thing, but when it comes to Rosemary ah I don't want to be involved" **Patricia:** "Why? Please tell us more about Rosemary?" **Rosemary's sister**: "Honestly speaking, Rosemary is not my young sister. We are not even related" **Me:** "what!!!!!!!!!!!! **Rosemary's sister:** "Yes, we are not. I found Rosemary being dumped at the river bank hid inside the reeds crying, when I went there to wash my clothes. I was afraid at first, but when I saw her, I fell in love with her. I took her and raised her until now. " **Me:** "But still you can take the dowry. You raised her as your own child, right?" **Rosemary's sister:** "Yes I did." **Me:** So you can take our money because you are still her mother. " **Rosemary's sister:** "Yoh Rosemary is terrifying and weird. She could spend three months sometimes not staying at home, but there at the dam. Thanks God now she is out of my life. I don't want to be stressed by bringing her back again. If I tell you more about her, you will be afraid of her and chase her away. Better to see it for yourselves. All my children suffered because of Rosemary. She drowned them in the dam after I had a fight with her. If you fight or argue with her or upsets, her, please don't go near water, you will see" **Patricia:** 'I don't fear that, I am a Christian and I believe in God. So no need to be afraid of those demons" Later we dismissed Rosemary's sister and us went pathways. Now all the truth about Rosemary was revealed to us. It's up to us to decide while they was still time. **Patricia:** "Brother, you heard it for yourself about your wife, what kind of monster she is. Break things with her before she brings any harm to our family. " I saw that Patricia didn't like Rosemary since day one; I told her everything about her. Now her hatred towards her was extreme inside her heart. "Sister calm down. You heard it also that she don't have relatives. So if we kicked her out what she would do? Let's try to help her so that what is happening to her grinds to halt. " **Patricia:** "Be careful brother to fall in love with a mermaid. I see that love blinded you. You heard her so-called sister that her children almost killed by Rosemary. Don't forget what happened to Keith. I don't like your wife at all Nigel. "She surrendered about Rosemary and gave me her portentous advice that no matter what happens the blame would be on me. To make her hatred worse, my aunt who stayed in Harare told her what Rosemary did at her place. In my heart, I loved Rosemary with my whole heart. Another thought came of separating with my relatives and find another place to stay elsewhere, where they cannot bother us anymore.

Everyday Patricia yells at Rosemary and fights over small things, and this made me felt sick in my guts. I knew my sister very well, when she was cross with a person, until death. Especially church days, she always yells at Rosemary, wanted her to go to church to get deliverance. If you don't want to get along with Rosemary, talk about church or praying. Church was her biggest enemy. Prince went to U.K. My sister refused to go, leaving me alone with Rosemary. She organized people who rent out house and I should go with her privately. Rosemary, when she will notice that we are gone, maybe she will go back to her relatives. But my heart was feeling pain to leave her, especially when I look at her, tears would break out uncontrollably. Rosemary saw that Patricia was her biggest enemy. One morning; she followed me outside the house and came to sit next to me. In morning there was more joy in the part of me that peeks through the windows of my eyes. In the morning there was more love awaiting a chance to jump into the air in that silent crackle we sense with our soul. In the morning there was more deep sweetness that resonates within and finds a way to express this energy that was me. **Me:** "Rosemary babes. I am your best friend, boyfriend, and your husband, right?" "Yes, Nigel you are and why saying that?"

She asked with a changed voice changed seemed disturbed about my question. "Why are you having so many secrets and hiding it from me? Are you here to waste my time or to destroy me or what Rosemary? Please tell me about your life what I should be supposed to know. " The lines on my face etched the story of a sad face. My crow's feet spoke of anger and the deep creases in my cheeks told of a man who have had enough. **Rosemary:** "Daddy, you know all my relatives, everything I told you. I don't have any secrets maybe you should tell me?" **Me:** "Don't get upset. I mean no harm at all. Okay, let's leave the topic. So tell me about the mermaid thing?" **Rosemary:** "What mermaid thing?" Nigel just say what you want to say. I know your tactics and plans......." She stood up being pissed off and started going inside the house yelling at me and left me talking to myself. **Me:** "I was trying to take your side, Rosemary." With my sister, our bond was so strong as concrete. We were now spending much time together than with Rosemary. She was spending most of the time home alone. Me and my sister we were not staying at home at all. In the morning, we go out then comes back in the evening. One day, we came back late around eleven midnight with Patricia. Rosemary was still awake in the blankets. We didn't greet each other; I got inside the blankets facing the opposite side covering my head with the blankets.

Rosemary was now out of my mind. Whenever I tried to ask her something, wanted to solve our problems, she could throw it on my face. Yelling at me and got angry easily..... no. no. no it was enough. Plus sex sometimes once or twice a month whenever she pleases. Her private part kept appearing and disappearing every time.... What kind of woman was that? **Rosemary:** "Nigel, you have changed since your sister arrived here. We used to be love birds, and I was feeling being dipped in the ocean of love. But now I can't see it anymore Patricia is bad-mouthing you right? I don't care about her hatred but what I know is that one day is one day" she kept talking, but I remained quiet then fallen asleep. This day I slept like a baby. Patricia was the one to wake me up. She wanted me to accompany her to the dam to wash blankets and some of her clothes. We put our blankets inside the boot and eased the car into gear, straight to the dam. Happiness is in everything; I dare you to invite it in. It is in the rain, cool and fresh, just as deeply as the sunshine, for they bring forth different emotions. Happiness is enjoying the moment, being present for that gift that is living, and allowing it to become intense. We arrived and parked the car 500 meters from the dam because they was a steep off slope down all the way to the dam. We took our blankets, and then started washing them being happy.

After, we put them on the rocks and thorny bushes to dry up, and then started swimming. Happy is what I felt when I was with Patricia, It's was not that she was fireworks and chatter; mostly she was so quiet. Just being near her lights me up inside, gives me a serenity I can never know without her being close. It's like the breath I take aren't full when she was away, like the smiles I smiled were incomplete somehow. Just being next to her was my favorite place in the world. It was her that creates the warmth in my soul, her that fills me full of love and keeps the fire burning in my eyes. If that isn't happiness I don't know what is, so I'll let it be my own definition, the one I kept with me always. We ended up playing this game of placing hands on small caves, catching small fish with our own hands. This day we caught many. We were now exhausted and sat on one rock near the dam talking.

Suddenly, a huge monstrous white snake came out from water with a rattling sound which filled the previously silent air. In that moment, there is no past or future. Every capacity of our brains focused on this horrific reptile before us. I was seeing its scale burned on my retina, its green steel eyes taking in my form, selecting possible place to bite, and its forked tongue savors our scent. Its body was like a frozen coil in the hot sun. It came out splashing water in the dam and fell on us as rain. All our blankets, which were about to be dry, became wet again. Patricia held my hand, finally; our legs agreed to move, slowly, retreating started heading to where our car was launched. Going up there was a steep off slope, meaning a rise and fall of the land surface, the elements of Topography. This steep required a person who was physically fit and having a good stamina to climb to the top. We didn't climbed far then stopped, and started looking backwards to see if the monster was still in pursuit. But was not moving, paused in one place with its eyes fixed on us, exposing its half body to the surface. Its eyes were huge and round.

As fear struck my bones, I fell down and started rolling back to the dam. Patricia screamed and ran quickly and stood me up before reaching the dam, and we started going up again from the start favoring my right leg which was in pain because of my fall. As we were about to finish the steep-off slope, a whirlwind appeared to where our car was coming against us to the death blowing violently. It rises up and blinds our eyes. Deafens our ears. Makes the whole place empty of substance. We tried to oppose it but it was too powerful. It was blowing on a high speed of blowing a car away... so what about a person?

Luckily, there were trees alongside the road, then climbed one on each of them. I find a branch that my short arms could reach. It wasn't long before I found one and was hoisting myself up into the tree. My heart was pounding and hands were sweating as I pulled myself higher and higher into the tree. Foot by foot, branch by branch, I reached higher and higher in the tree. How scary, it was to be this high up! To be safe my sister's tree, which she was climbing on, blown away by its roots. Tears streamed out as I saw my sister in the air being thrown in the dam. She was thrown a meter away to where the monstrous snake was. *Oh God, please help; she is my sister, mother, and father.... don't let her die Lord.* I prayed with tears, seeing her struggling for her life increased my passion.

That snake didn't move but was staring at me with Patricia underneath it, a step closer to her that would be her end. She tried to swim to end but this rushing wind kept pulling her back to the middle of the dam. "Nigel, help me brother I am dying' she called for help to a person who was in the middle of nowhere, my wire was mixed up upstairs. I felt pain in my heart and body, another thought was saying... run call for help but the other was telling me to save my sister. *But if I come back seeing her dead?* Lastly, I saw it was better to die with my sister. When I was closer to reach her, that snake started advancing towards me. When I stopped, it would do the same... It was like I was the prey not Patricia. So I was stuck at the same place not knowing what to do. Patricia kept calling for help. **Patricia:** "Rosemary let off go me please," she said, asking Rosemary to let her go... Rosemary was the one who helped me that day when I was in danger, also helped those two girls who were captured by mermaids. I saw that it was better to collect her maybe she could help Patricia. As I started running, Patricia screamed again. "Nigel, please.... don't leave me, brother. " I went back again trying to help her but that monstrous snake became more furious because I kept coming. It came closer to me with its tongue flipped out in the air to taste fear. This time it was coming after me without stopping. "Nigel run, go home," said Patricia she saw that if not that I was a dead person. I ran, feet kissing the land. Perhaps I would have balked at the idea of running so far and fast, I relished the prospect. These feet were made to travel at a speed and as a light at the paws of a lion. Covering no distance, I heard Patricia screaming loud. Then I checked and saw this snake was advancing to its meal. Suddenly, appeared big fishes with the sizes of human and started battling with the snake. Some surrounded Patricia. She gave me a sign to keep going and call people for help. Running was my thing. I was not sure if my sister was still alive. *Patricia was my everything... oh God help me, please....*

CHAPTER TEN

Even if someone hailed me whilst running, I couldn't hear a thing. I was travelling miles per hour. With all the thorns of the road as I was barefoot, I didn't hear them piercing, my flesh. I was covered in bloody sweat all over me. I arrived at the door breathing heavily and it was locked meaning that there was someone inside. Obvious Rosemary. I knocked many times, but no one opened it. *Why is Rosemary still sleeping this hour?* "Rosemary, Rosemary," I yelled calling her name but to no avail, no one answered. I rushed around the house, but our bedroom was built in the midst where there was no window for me to look inside. I came back at the door, with all my potential I banged the door over and over repeatedly, "Rosemary, Rosemary, Rosemary, answer, wake up please" I scurried to the kitchen window and picked up some few small rocks and blasted into it. The window knocked together and squashed into small pieces on the floor with a vicious vibration. It fell into pieces and luckily; there were no burglar bars, so it was easy for me to get inside. I rumbled to the bedroom and guess what!!! Rosemary was lying on the floor, wearing her private clothes with water covering her full body and the whole floor. *Water again??* **Me:** "Rosemary, Rosemary, what is wrong with you?" I asked frankly. I recalled what she did at aunt's place, and she rejected all. now I had caught her in the act. She tried to stand up and fell down to the ground, then started crying touching her legs. She seemed to be in pain. "My God, oh my G...." I said rubbing my bewildered head and commenced rubbing it, "Rosemary what is happening?"

Rosemary: "Nigel, help me, "she added with her voice, which was low like a person who is dying. For sure she was in agony; I lifted her from the floor and placed her on the bed. Remember Patricia was still in trouble, I came here for help from Rosemary and now she was the one who was in need of mine as well. I saw it was better to solve Patricia's matter first. As I was to go to outside to look for someone who I can go with to the dam, Rosemary screamed again touching her stomach, "Nigel my legs please, my stomach ooh.." her body was sweating a lot, mourning in real pain. My sister was in the midst of the dam surrounded by monsters and now!! Shock and confusion looped around in my mind until there was no room for everything else. I was now residing in hell from one day to the next. But there is nothing I could do to escape. I don't know where I would go if I did. I feel utterly powerless, and that feeling is my prison. I entered my own free will; I locked the door, and I threw away the key. *Lord why you have forsaken me and put me in these horrible difficult questions?* It was only questions but no one to answer them. My eyes kept staring at Rosemary, who was pointing her legs saying that they were not moving at all.

Touching them, their temperature was as cold as fridge temperature. **Rosemary:** "Daddy, Daddy, help me to go to the toilet, oh my stomach." I rushed with her straight to the toilet and made her to sit on her own. She fell again on her face and started screaming." Nigel, why are you hurting me? Don't go, anyway. Please stay with me." If someone gave me food that day, no amount of chewing made it possible to swallow. My mouth was drier than a sandbox in summer. Quickly, I lifted her back to sit nicely. I leaned her nicely so that she wouldn't fall. Her eyes marveled me; it was changed to blue. That wasn't the color of her eyes. "Babe, please be strong right. I will call for an ambulance to come now. Stay where you are. don't move until I am back. " I rushed outside and heard her screaming, trying to stop me," no, no, no, Nigel come back please I am dying" I didn't looked back, went straight to the police station.

On my was I was trying to call the ambulance but my phone was off. I switched it on, but the screen was turning black. Strange because last night I charged it and the battery was full. So why not coming on? I saw that it was disturbing my pace; I put it back inside the pocket and proceed with my thing. You know police camps in rural areas are not that busy; it was a single room with few policemen. People were queuing outside to get help. Some were seated seemed exhausted of standing for long. To be honest, I was very impatient to wait in long queues. However, I felt furious to see such one. I saw that it would take over four hours for my turn to arrive if I follow the line. This made me skip the line and went straight to where the police officer was assisting people. People started complaining that I should go back to the line, but I didn't listen to any of them. My disrespectful characteristics bothered the police officer and started knocking my head with his stick, which was painful. **Police Officer:** "Hey you young man, where is your honors? These people you see are also in a hurry as you, maybe your case in not even important than theirs. So go back to the line" his voice was so loud and deep which aroused my fear from the dead. Since my young age, I was afraid of the cops. Time was moving, and to follow the queue it was a total waste of time. I ran to the location nearby where I knew a certain old man who could help me. Luckily, he was available. I told him my story in short and he took his weapons, dogs and his young son then started rushing to the dam. Within minutes, we were at the dam. we arrived where we parked our car with Patricia with my eyes fixed to the dam. After the steep-off slope, we were at the dam. Beloved, they was silence lay like a down-filled duvet over the area, muffling the slightest sound and creating an atmosphere of total tranquility. The quietness was almost tangible. We saw nothing or a sign that something happened before, none. Our blankets were all dried up. I was puzzled by this moment, shock wrapped my body. I heard drops of sweat streaming on my eyebrows a cold sweat broke out again on my forehead and I mopped it away with my forearm.

People I was with kept staring at me with that saying eye saying, *how far brother?* I knew that my sister was dead though I wanted to cry but I hold myself. A person who is captured by mermaids if you cry, she will die. I tried to be strong not to shed tears the old man asked me to explain in detail what happened but that power of moving my lips was no longer found in me. Again I left Rosemary alone. she was in pain. I don't know what happened after I left. More and more stress fell upon me. *Why did I leave Patricia at the first place? It was better to die alongside my sister and now she is gone. Now Prince is in London, whom should I tell my problems?* Another splash of stress felt upon me.

All these questions kept running inside my head without answers. People I was with started hovering around, searching everywhere maybe they could find anything solidarity. I was left alone being heartbroken and stressed. *Where is my sister? Maybe Rosemary died also!!* This was too much for a young child as I was to handle. The old man came back and told me to explain everything to the police while they still had time. At first I wanted to commit suicide by throwing myself in the dam, so I should follow my sister. But this old man knew that leaving me alone was not a good idea, I would do something stupid. He held my hand so I should stand on my feet. When he was busy doing that, dogs started barking, they saw something and started running towards that side. The old man rushed with his dogs followed by his son, and I was left alone. Suddenly, I heard something getting inside the dam behind me, splashing water everywhere. I was disturbed and shaken a little and stand, then looked back to see what it was. They was nothing only water was moving up and down all sides of the dam, emphasizing that there was something took a dive.

Maybe it was that snake I thought, now I was not scared anymore, the damage was already done. I closed my eyes so that when it comes to swallowing me, I will not see a thing. A while passed, nothing happened. I opened them again and something strange caught with my eyes. I saw a reflecting in transitory brightness, glare, glow, blaze of lights, dazzling, bright, and dim-white figure coming out of the water and started following where the old man rushed. What disturbed me from having a clear look was the reflection of this monstrous being... I remained at my spot with no fear in me, *whatever comes I am here*. A minute passed the old man was not returning, even his dogs were not barking at all. In the middle of my thoughts, I heard footsteps of a person coming toward me though I tried harder to ignore them but it kept coming closer and closer. When it was near me, it stopped exactly behind me. I became furious and lifted a big stone and thrown it to where it was hearing them coming, with all mighty power. To my surprise, there was no person or anything. Not even a sign that maybe that person run away whilst I was facing the opposite. Now this got my attention. I couldn't breathe; it felt as if someone was choking me for a minute.

My heart was racing, and all I wanted to do was to curl up into a ball and wait for someone to save me. But no one would, no one was there. It seemed as if it was the end of the road for me. As I was looking around to find who was walking, the old man called me. He was waving his hand for me to come and have a look. Quickly without hesitation, I rushed there so fast and what a huge surprise................. I saw Rosemary lying on the rock and Patricia on the ground, coughing out water. Rosemary was looking exhausted like a person who has worked so much. My face was washed blank with confusion, like my brain cogs couldn't turn fast enough to take in the information from my wide eyes. Every muscle in my body just froze before a grin crept onto my face; it soon stretched from one side to the other showing every single tooth. I scrunch my eyes tight, maybe it could be my mind playing tricks with me, but the result was still the same. Confusing both with happiness fell upon me though I wasn't believing what I was seeing. Rosemary, I left her home sick being to death. How come she is here? What happened/

how did she know? I glued my eyes on them with these questions circling in my head. My gaze fell like an act of violence; a glare to stop my heart, though I was jovial to see my sister being alive, the old man was busy sucking out water from her lungs. He started going to the dam to refresh for he has done a huge job. "Come here, my brother," said Patricia, standing on her own two feet. 'Where is Rosemary Nigel?"

Me: "What happened?" I asked her giving her a warm hug. But she remained quiet. What she was asking was Rosemary, whom she was drinking water at the dam. **Patricia:** "Your wife saved me" she added going where Rosemary was launched with her arms wide open so that she could give her a hug. Rosemary also came to meet her halfway then grabbed each other and the old man smiled. Their hug was simple enough gesture affection, perhaps the fragile beginnings of love between these two. But Patricia I know hate Rosemary with her heart, so where is this love coming from? To me, I was in total confusion trying to add these things up. The old man told us that it was time to go home and he started leading the way. I grabbed my sister, then started going to the car. Rosemary, she said she will follow later.

She wanted to take a bath. "No, no, no, Rosemary, I won't leave you here alone, mermaids will capture you. You are going with us," said Patricia, who refused to her alone. Lastly, she agreed to go with us. The car was being driven very fast with the speed of lightning bolt. We arrived, and I rushed inside the house, straight to the toilet where I left Rosemary, maybe I could see real Rosemary. But there was no one. I rumbled to the bedroom and saw there was no water on the floor, everything was dry. *I left Rosemary in the toilet, unable to move, and in the bedroom was water everywhere, and then I saw her at the dam with Patricia. Impossible...* Then I started walking into the dining room and saw Patricia sitting on the couch. Rosemary was preparing tea for us.

CHAPTER ELEVEN

I took a hush moment with my head, which was about to explode with confusion. What I needed to perceive was who Rosemary? The person I left behind at home and now she showed up at the Dam. How come? I glanced at Patricia and asked her to tell me the whole story, but Rosemary was the one insisted to tell me, "I will tell you the daddy the whole story, Patricia she's not recalling anything. She is in total blur, Daddy. She particularly remembers when she saw me saving her" added Rosemary, speaking on her behalf. Oh ok, I don't want to quarrel anymore I went to the shops to play snooker and both to clear my head was about to boiling with confusion. In the middle of playing, I heard noise of wheels Wheeling and Patricia called my name to come where she was. It was Patricia's car I abandoned what I was doing and moved to meet her inside the car. A moment of silence passed without speaking to each other. **Patricia**: "brother I come to tell what happened to me and what I was experiencing in the water but I'm failing to remember every detail" she was squeezing her head so that maybe she could remember some part of it, "sorry brother I remember nothing" she said with an upset in her beautiful face.

I am a person who doesn't forget easily, but I don't see if my memory is still serving me well. Seriously, though I don't know what is going on, maybe we should go home and try to have a nap maybe I could wake up getting it. We went home and Rosemary was cooking food for us but Patricia went straight forward to her room then slept leaving the two of us alone. And what I wanted to ask Rosemary but me completely forgot. Daddy, I assumed you loved me but you don't have care with me. I needed to respond at first, but I zipped my mouth then she goes ahead with her story, really Nigel leaving me alone in this very house but you saw that I was dying" My anger was roused and reacted, " if you were dying, how come I saw you at the dam? And how do you know that Patricia was missing? Who are you Rosemary? I asked with a loud indignant voice. " I want you to know this that mysterious takes long to unfold that's the truth always has its ways to come out" **Rosemary**: "Where all this anger coming from without even hearing the full story let me conclude she added with an intense voice which was on top of mine? Daddy please, I am asking you to listen first the whole story, and then you may say all you need. What took place to me of being sick the way you saw me earlier happened before. And I know the cure to alleviate this disease found in the river bank. So when you left me alone, I strengthened myself to be strong, and went to the dam to pick up some medicine. Luckily, it was there; I took it then drink it and within minutes I was fine. I mean it healed me completely, so on my way back.

That's where I saw Aunty Patricia in the middle of the dam with a mermaid under her. I hate to see people drowning or being attacked by mermaids and do nothing about it. I dove inside the water daddy and the Mermaid wanted to attack me at first but it failed. Then I rescued Aunty Patricia and came out of the dam. That's what happened Daddy nothing else" she said going to the bathroom, showing that she wanted no more questions. II felt my head spinning. I followed her to the bedroom, and she was already in the blankets. **Me**: "Rosemary tell me what do you really do? I don't know who you are anymore I don't even know who my wife really is. I said looking to where she was lying. She looked at me with her strange eyes for a while saying nothing.

Rosemary: " Nothing Nigel, I'm only your wife that's what I know and why asking like that go straight to your point?" I saw that she's trying to hide everything from me she was getting angry for nothing instead of me to be angry, " tell me everything I supposed to know or else I will kick you out of my house. Now! Wake up and pack your bags now" I made up my decision, no matter what she must go. I started dragging out of the bed. "Auntie Patricia wake up and see what Nigel is doing. He is beating me and kicking me out of the house. Come auntie" **Patricia**: " nonsense... Nigel shut up) what are you doing. She's not going anywhere but you are the one who's going to be kicked out of this house." she said coming from her room with her big bug-eyed eyes wide opening. She took Rosemary and went together to her room. They left me alone, and I knew that for sure Rosemary's did something to my sister. I went back inside the blankets then fallen asleep, once fallen asleep I started to dream again, but this time I was a worm on a fish line hook used to catch mermaids. Those people were fishing me was Patricia and Rosemary. I saw big fishes and mermaids coming after me, this made me to scream loudly trying to free myself. Rosemary pulled the fishing line out of the dam.

When Patricia saw that I was out of the water she fell down with laughter and instructed Rosemary to put me back again. On and on again many times, all fish and mermaids started tearing my body into half, how painful it was though I was trying to fight back throwing my legs into the air. I scream from deep within those forces its way from my mouth; it is as if my terrified soul has unleashed a demon. This nightmare was more of a night terror, because it feels as if I might die from the pain in my brain. I was desperately trying to wake up. I woke up from this nightmare with my heart pounding very fast like a group of people was pounding Rapoko from the field. I sat down with this anger towards Rosemary, another mind was saying... *follow her to Patricia's room and beat her up.* But that power was no longer in me. Another thought of putting poison in her food came up. *Definitely, she must die; she said that she fights mermaids... where all that power was coming from?* I became frustrated until I felt asleep. Boom! Comes again the dream.

This time I was locked inside the cage underwater, and mermaids were trying to break the cage to feast on me. On top of me was Rosemary sitting on a large rock and Patricia the other side. I wept hard; calling their names for help, and Patricia wanted to come for rescue but was prevented by Rosemary who kept piercing her with a reed stick. All water turned into blood because of Patricia's blood. My screaming was violence in the air, a way to take the pain and transfer the tension in the air. "No Rosemary, I swear if you hurt my sister, I am coming for you. Rosemary, Ro..." I woke up screaming at Rosemary and saw Patricia standing at the bedroom door staring at me with their hands folded. "I heard you calling my name," said Patricia coming to the bed and sat on it. I remained silent and went to the dining room and switched on the television. Soon both of them followed me up and asked me what I was dreaming because I was looking disturbed.

I remained quiet and my eyes met with Rosemary and we stared at each other for a while without blinking. Patricia asked me for the second time, but no reply was coming from me .My ignorance frustrated her and went back to sleep followed by Rosemary. I did not go to sleep until dawn watching geographic channel on dstv. I was still going with my plan of getting rid of Rosemary. The sun rises as a canopy of gold, bright amid the blue, bidding the stars to take their nightly rest. As darkness surrenders, every color changes from tinges of charcoal to vibrancy. There are days I wonder what we give in return for such gifts of divine magic, what a frightful new day. Patricia woke up, went to bath, then after changing clothes she came to where I was with her bags packed. **Me** "Where are you going sister in these early hours, and what are all these bags for?" **Patricia**: "Brother, they called me to come to work this morning. They said something urgent came up, so they are cutting my leave days. So I have no time. Walk me to the taxi rank I want to catch 10; 30 flight. Let's go we will talk on the way. " What! She was behind time. I thought she still has more days. When we were at the gate, Rosemary followed us and took one bag. I thought I will talk with my sister about my problems on the way, now Rosemary follows again. People got insights into what was bothering them, but they could hardly did anything for the damn situation to change. Rosemary's presence bothered me. We arrived at the taxi rank, the rank marshal was taunting, and only one person left who is in a hurry. She boarded and waved us through the window. Tears flows rapidly, I Was going to miss my sister. 'Ha ha ha... Nigel are you sure you are crying. "Rosemary laughed at me and this made me cry even more. I couldn't hold my tears, people were at the taxi rank noticed i was crying and all their eyes were on me, such an embarrassment for a person like me to cry for someone but I wasn't caring. We walked back home and Rosemary was trying to make me laugh by her unfunny jokes but I didn't laugh any of it. I wasn't being offended by all the dumb blonde jokes but because of her. We arrived, and I went straight to the bedroom and tried to sleep but couldn't because of too much stress.

I was still planning to go ahead with my plan of killing Rosemary, *but what I would say what killed her to the police? If they find me guilty and go to jail? Others are all in U. K. Even if I run... it was a sin against God"* Indeed Rosemary came to destroy my life. This time I bit more than I can chew. I need a shoulder to cry on..... They was a friend of mine called Nathan. I visited him for ideas, how happy he was to see me after a long time. **Nathan:** "It's a great surprise to get visited by you, Nigel. I thought you had dashed me? Is your wife telling you not to visit and play with your friends? Nathan was a witty person who was funny for the opposite reason: those people who say things that are funny and also very smart. Witty people are also quick with their jokes." He tried even to crack his best jokes, but not this time, I wasn't in the mood of laughing. **Nathan:** "ha ha-ha why bringing your long sad face here? Did your wife break up things with you? **Ha. Ha. Ha** the laughter continues. I told you not to rush to marry; women are trouble makers. Now you are stressed... You are stressed Nigel. " Nathan was giving me more stress. He asked me to accompany him to their field to get maize cobs. We reached a small stream with little water and he jumped and when it comes my turn; I felt scared and saw this stream as a big river. He looked back and saw I wasn't coming and asked me what the problem is. I told him what was worrying me and eating me inside.

When he heard about Rosemary acting like a mermaid, he laughed at me, " so what is the problem having a mermaid wife? This is more than amazing Nigel, it's astonishing. Do not leave her; it's a blessing because you will be rich. "Really Nathan, that's the solutions you are giving me? Bye I am going home, I can't take this anymore "Nathan's silly ideas upsets me and I went back home. Days and weeks passed, leaving with Rosemary. She was no longer sleeping at home many of the days. People were telling me they were seeing her at the dam alone in water. Now she was showing her true colors that she was a sea monster. When she wasn't around, I planned to kick her out of the house but once she arrives, all those thoughts will vanish and started loving her so much. But once she was at the dam, I even blamed my foolishness decision of staying with her. One day, I remembered my brother Prince then started beeping him an endless time until he called back.

I told him everything about what was Rosemary doing. He asked me to tell Patricia then hung the phone. To tell Patricia? Obvious she will take Rosemary's side; it was better not to tell her. Days passed Rosemary staying at the dam. When I go there to find out myself, I will see nothing only birds and ducks, but others will do. One day Patricia called in the middle of the night wanted to talk to Rosemary. It was a chance given to expose her to Patricia. Instead, she said I was abusing her. That's why she was running away from me and staying outside.

She blew it on my face, what kind of sister she was? Because of Rosemary's scarce times, I was spending more time at the church seeking deliverance. Pastor saw that my problem was enormous, and asked me to come with her for deliverance. I persuaded her many times, but it all goes in vain, she refused. Prince was calling almost daily checking up on me. To my situation he said he would come out with a plan, but the days and weeks passed doing nothing. Patricia was now under Rosemary's spell. Every time she calls wants to speak with Rosemary not me, I was her biggest enemy. When we talk about Rosemary we ended up throwing bitter words at each other. One way to get high blood pressure is to go mountain climbing over molehills. I kept pressuring Prince until he bought me a flight ticket to London without Rosemary or Patricia's knowledge. Before the day for me to go to U.K., Rosemary came from the dam and spend the whole day together but my mind was already in U.K.

No one talked to another, lastly I was going to leave her for good, No more problems from Rosemary. One thing was worrying me was, how to sneak out without being seen. I wanted her to find the place empty, *but if she finds out what I will say I was going?* Even chance to pack my clothes wasn't available; she was monitoring the entire house. I took a few clothes and wrapped them inside a black plastic and disguised myself as I was going to dump them in the garbage bin. When I was at bin, I hid them behind the bin so that on my way out I will come and collect them here; it was easy for me. My heart missed a beat. I thought maybe Rosemary was going to see me in act. When I was back inside the house, I saw Rosemary holding my passport saying nothing. I Left her with it but my gut was twisting, what she was doing with it? Moments later she placed it down and went to sleep.

As her consciousness ebbed, her mind went into free fall, swirling with the beautiful chaos of a new dream. I saw that now she was miles away. I waved my hand in front of her eyes to see if she would notice anything. Nothing she kept snoring. Quickly, I packed my clothes inside another plastic and hid them outside. Then, bathed and changed so that when tomorrow comes, it will be easy for me. I will just wake up and go, everything was planned so nicely. I went to sleep saying my silent last goodbyes to Rosemary. My 5 o'clock alarm was on. I started dreaming on a plane going to London. At the airport, I was welcomed by Rosemary then took my bags and started leading the way as I was a newcomer. Instead, we started going underneath the dam where they were all kinds of fish.

We arrived where crocodiles and other sea monsters was launched then disappeared, leaving me alongside beasts. I tried hard to escape by swimming hard, but it all gone in vain. You can't escape water animals by swimming. I could swim forever, dive forever, and be here in this underwater world forever. There is something about the motion of it that becomes natural after a while. I'll always need the air and the sunlight, to feel the saline water wash over my skin and through my eyelashes. I screamed hard calling Prince to come. These monsters didn't harm me; they kept circling me around. Luckily, I was saved from my nightmares by 5 o'clock alarm. I wake the way kings wake, just the same. We are all blessed with the same time, the same experience of consciousness. My eyes greet the day shine, my heart and lungs expand. There are times that I feel that I must have been so blessed to live the same day over and over, even though I age, even few moments are so identical.

This day was a special day for me. I took my passport and my wallet and placed them inside my right pocket. I looked at Rosemary oh God. *What is this now?* She was lying on her back and her stomach was big, round and shining, seemed about to explode. Her blouse was torn in half by this big stomach. She was laying lifeless. Her auburn hair was scattered in multiple places. Her emerald green- brownish eyes were wide open, but her jade irises held a sudden sadness. And the smell. The smell was the most disturbing thing I had ever sniffed. It was a blatant her bowels had been released, and all too soon. My heart pounded as one question continued to race through my mind. *What happened?* I tried to wake her up by tapping her back, but she wasn't responding even a bit. Touching her body was freezing as an ice-ocean. I tried to wake her repeatedly with disbelief on my face but the result was the same. Prince called, I failed to answer it because I was wrapped in shock.

Lastly, I ignored Rosemary's situation and started to proceed with my journey to U.K. A rotten meat odor started coming out from

Rosemary and then I stopped instantly at the verandah. This smell shivered me. It was a scent as old as the world. It was a hundred aromas of a thousand places. It was the tang of pine needles. It was the musk of sex. It was the muscular rot of mushrooms. It was the spice of oak. Meaty and redolent of soil and bark and herbs. It was bats and husks and burrows and moss. It was solid and alive - so alive! A disgusting smell. Immediately, Black clouds sprawl across the sky, billowing in from the west. Their brassy glare drains color from houses and trees and burnished cars in driveways, leaving neighborhoods tinted bronze in the faltering light. The air grows heavy, and the humidity presses down, suffocating. The scent of rain is dark and heady. A stillness falls over the street, and in the silence comes a low crackle of thunder, rolling across rooftops to the patterning of tiny raindrops. For a moment, everything stops. Even the wind holds its breath. A streak of hot silver splits the sky, and the downpour begins. Soon the whole yard was covered in small flash floods. Ah! God where this cyclone Rosemary was coming from?

The stress spread through my mind like ink on paper. I took in a deep, ragged breath before placing my hands, enclosed together, on my head. I ran back inside to check up on her for the third time and to check if she was breathing but was no pulse. The corpse was almost devoid of skin and pitted by burrowing insects. Riley turned away as her stomach heaved, nostrils filled with the smell of rotting meat. Her milky brown eyes stared into the frozen sky while the lipless mouth hung open. Though I was young, but I saw that Rosemary was dead, but why? She wasn't not even sick? That was my only question. Ngrr ngrr... phone alert **me**: Hello. ”

Prince: “Nigel, your ticket cost me a lot, if you miss your flight, that's it. I will help you again no more. Where are you now? Are you on your way to the airport? Hello!! Nigel, I said where you are?” I removed the phone slowly, slowly from my ear and cut the call without a reply. Tears fall in my heart like the rain on the town. Tears are nature's lotion for the eyes. The eyes see better for being washed by them. Crying was better because I was furious and can't do anything about it because I've run into a dead end. Rosemary was laying lifeless on the bed; even if I go to U.K. people will say who killed Rosemary? Obvious me because they think I run away. What will Patricia say? I sat on the floor obsessed and wish my parents if they were alive...

CHAPTER TWELVE

I heard my head spinning. I took my phone to call Prince, but I did not have that strength to speak. With this intense silence, somehow I screamed with my whole body. The eyes wide with horror, the mouth rigid and open, and my chalky face gaunt and immobile, the fists clenched with blanched knuckles tears playing its factor. *What would the police say?* Even to tell Patricia about this, I saw it was the worst idea. Time was ticking quickly, and Prince would have been waiting to hear that I was flying now. I went to the dining room and was water everywhere on the floor with pieces of green fresh reeds in it and small fish jumping. I thought this is the result of rainfall; it was causing water to flood in continuous stream of floods it started raining early this morning and hasn't let up since, the cars' roofs were dancing in spairy and I could hear the murmuring of the rain through the window. I grabbed my phone to call the police but then slipped down and dropped into the water. I picked it up and put it on and refused to come on. For the second time there I go again but still isn't turning on.

I went into the bedroom to use Rosemary's phone but it was switched off. I switched it on, but it was not turning on. This marveled me because our phones charged the whole night and the batteries were full. I tried to charge it but was not showing t charging. When the frustration builds and I think I might explode - I took a deep breath. I want to shout, have a tantrum and beat my hands on the ground like a toddler. I want to vent, let it out, but I don't want to say words I don't mean, be hurtful. It's just so easy to be cruel in that moment and then the damage is done, trying to figure out on how to deal with this situation. Ash, I sat down holding my jaw. I started to blame myself saying, i was wrong with my plan of fleeing Rosemary, But what I should do? Rosemary was a monster, and she didn't want to tell me the truth about herself. The rotten smell continues showing that her body was real bad without even a single day.

Unbelievable! I took my umbrella and volunteered to go to the police, *but will I say what killed her? Will they believe my alibi she wakes up dead and my hands were clean?* Rosemary was my first love and now. From this day I started to hate what they called love. Then I walked out of the house and wore my gumboots and went to the police. The rain was pouring little harder. I walked fast and put the umbrella on top of my head to protect myself from the rain.

Then the rain drops became bigger every second. Pitter patter, pitter patter it continues raining. My face was lazy because of stress, now and I was afraid that they would say I am the one who murdered her. I approached the police and handed them my case. We got into the car and went home. One of the policemen was told to take care of me. They assumed maybe I will run away. Softly splashing water droplets hit the car windows as we drive onwards. The skies are overhung with a blanket of grey, so much so that I can barely tell the difference between the sky and clouds. Despite car rides feeling tedious, the rain commonly calms me - I watch raindrops race down to the windows. And this caused us to be delayed.

We got to the house being followed by the police. Slowly, I turned the door handle of the main door. Something caught me with a surprise.... Rosemary was mopping water on the floor, seemed safe and sound. I jumped in the air as if a firecracker had gone off, shrieked, wild eyed, bewildered, hands over mouth, nostrils flaring, blood drained from face, mouth opening and shutting like a goldfish with no sound coming out, still as a statue, ridged as a board, face stuck in an incredulous expression, unblinking stare, shaking head in disbelief, sent reeling backwards, brain desperately scrambling to make sense of it all, rendered speechless, temporarily incapacitated, stood as if paralyzed from the neck up, gibbering nonsense, unable to comprehend what my eyes was showing me. Was she not dead? Police officer: "Hey, young boy, don't stand at the entrance you are blocking traffic. Show us the deceased we want to do our job. " They mixed me up and remained silent, not knowing what to say.

The other policeman was already lusting to Rosemary. He was glaring at her with bedroom eyes; he thought she was my sister. "Hey young man? Where is the dead body? We are running a tight schedule?" He added with a deep, scary voice. This injected a very effective dosage of fear into my system. I pointed him Rosemary, whom she was busy with the other policeman who was asking for numbers. I confused him what I was referring to. When I heard about the other policeman begging Rosemary's cell phone numbers, I got myself involved in their conversation and was the one who gave him her numbers. Rosemary's actions stressed me, so it was better if he took her or even for a zero price. But I'm frustrated the other police officer with me about wasting their vulnerable time. Many thoughts flooded my mind saying; *tell them I was playing officers.* Some were saying, *tell them Nigel that the one who is dead is the one you are asking phone contacts.* But I already told them that her body was already smelling. Then I took my phone and tried to turn it off and turned on. It was the time Prince was calling. I just left the room and left Rosemary with the police and went outside to answer the call. **Me:** "Prince Hello" **Prince:** "Nigel, where are you now? Are you at the airport?" I just kept quiet, and this made my brother to become angry. "I'm asking you. Where the hell are you now?" **Me:** "No brother at home, they are some....." Without letting me finish' **Prince:** You see Nigel. That's why people don't help you. Why you didn't come today?" **Me** "Rosemary wake up being dead, smelling. So i...." Again................

Prince: "Why? Oh God, what has happened, Nigel? Where is she now? " **Me:** "Prince is a ......" he immediately cut the call. Then I tried to call him on the phone to finish the story, but his phone was saying *the user busy.* I just got into the house with the police. I once thought I should pretend to be crazy and the police would leave me and go but how to do it was the problem. Then I took courage and told them the truth about the situation. But they didn't believe it and laughed at the thought of I was playing. Aar: they saw that I was not laughing but serious. "Hey young fella, maybe you think maybe we are the same age as you. I'm afraid that you are mistaken. Don't play with the cops. Arrest him, he will tell us his story at the station, "said the chief of the police ordering the other policeman. Cops was my biggest fear and especially to get beaten by them. We drove to the police station and questioned me why I was pranking them and my motive for doing it.

I kept talking about the girl and that she had died. The policeman then smacked at me with a big slap on the face so badly between the eyes I saw the darkness and Rosemary at the same time. The slap was as loud as a clap and stung my face. It had been an open-handed smack and it had left a red welt behind. Just below my eye was a small cut where the ring had caught me. I staggered backwards, clutching my face, eyes watering. It was painful and started to wipe my eyes, which was streaming tears of pain. He asked again, at first I wanted to act like a crazy mad-person but how to act like that. I gave them the same answer. He laughed and gave me another shot his slap didn't hurt me but me saw him rubbing his cheek, the same cheek right cheek he slapped me to show that it was in pain. He then became more aggressive, exuded an animosity that was like acid - burning, slicing, potent. His face was red with suppressed rage. He laid me down on my stomach then took a button stick and rammed me one shot to the buttocks. Instead of feeling pain none, he throws his button stick away, favoring his buttocks, jumping the entire room, squeezing them up again and again. He was in pain. We both scared puzzled about this incident because I was the one being beating but he was the one feeling pain. The officer came inside to find out what I had said, but he was told that I had not told them anything. Sergeant got angry. "So you think it's a play are here? You killed a person only; they are no such thing to report things which is not there. If we beat you nicely, you will spit everything."

Then he took that button stick on the ground. "You see this; it is the punishment of fools. The truth lies within this stick, stand up and come here," he said the sergeant and grabbed my head and put it between his legs and bent me in half. I closed my eyes with tears streaming rapidly. I kept my eyes closed, waiting to hear the smash. I heard the real loud sound like a balloon which blown up on my back. I saw sergeant pushing me away from him, holding his back scrubbing it over again and again jumping the whole room. He felt more pain than I knew a human body could bare. Other policemen laughed with their mouths closed, hiding their laughter from their chief looking the opposite direction. Though I was in total blur about what was taking place, it was now not surprising; I just knew it was Rosemary's doings. **Sergeant,** "Tell us what you did and stop wasting our time?" said the chief office beating me several times with the button stick, but still he was the victim to pain. He threw the stick away and went outside. They locked me up in a private room for a while until I had fallen asleep.

When I woke up, I searched for my phone but didn't find it until I realized the police took it. *What did Prince will do? He quickly hangs the call before I finish talking. Why does Rosemary not following me to the police station? She sees me being loaded in the jeep with the police and know?* I asked my question but no one answered. I sat there and heard the door open. I looked at the person and saw Rosemary coming in. Me: "Rosemary, are you a policeman? Where did you find keys or you get along with one policeman?" I asked her, but she did not answer me and she grabbed me by the hand and we walked out. We passed through the room where police offices were and sheriffs we didn't greet them, actually; I don't know if they saw us. We walked out holding hands like we are coming out of a five-star hotel, but with many questions in my head. At the gate, I felt my hand which I was holding with Rosemary's hand become free, swinging back and forth. I just looked at Rosemary but I did not see her. I stopped and thought maybe she went somewhere, but there was no sign of her coming back. I started to walk slowly maybe she could catch me before I arrived home. *The police will look at me. I am now a fugitive.* I came home and saw Rosemary lying asleep. I gazed at her without moving my eyes from her then woke her up. She seemed she was miles away in deep sleep with her red eyes, which was a faithful witness that for sure she was sleeping. Ash I wondered, *so which Rosemary I see at the police station.*

Maybe I am hallucinating, but if I am how come I come here? I said let me ask her, where did she go from the gate because I was waiting for her all the way. "Go where?" she asked being surprised with my question. "From that police station," I added. "Since morning I was here.

I didn't go anywhere Nigel. " I just kept quiet because I got used to her strange deeds. "Nigel, they is something that I would like to show you out there like now" she said wearing her pants and grabbed me by the hand and pulled me out. At first I thought she wanted to show me something in the yard until we were outside the gate. "Where are we going to Rosemary?" I asked, but she just said let us go. There we go facing the direction to the dam and felt my conscience had fallen and my heart pounding. I knew very well that I was in trouble. I wanted to refuse, but I did not have the power to speak or argue, my tears started streaming on my poor cheeks. I knew that my case of running away she knows it.

I was going to be punished only... I did not know what to say or do. Rosemary realized that my tears were flowing out but seemed uncaring and had nothing to say. She walked away quietly. I just sat down and Rosemary standing up commanding me to keep on moving with a serious, angry face. "Rosemary why you are doing all this to me? What wrong did I do to you?" I was crying out showing sadness that maybe she would be kind and have mercy on me. Instead, she laughed and said, "Stand up, Daddy, did I say you have wronged me?" At the water I knew the story, though I wanted to refuse continue going there, but my strength was so weak. She pulled my hand, and I got up and started walking wiping my tears like a little baby. My plan of running away now trapped me in real shit with Rosemary and I don't know what aware her plans or what she would do with me at the dam. I draw a cross my finger on my head and shoulders and started communicating with God. "God *you are the owner of all these things. Why did you give me such a person? Others you bless them is this the blessing?*"

I prayed silently in my heart. We came to the dam and sat down on a rocky rock was near water. We sat down staring at this deadly dam and its blue deep water, which was scary to look at. No one was at the dam only Crocodiles, deer, ducks, baboons and birds were only visible at the other side of the river bank. "Daddy, take my phone and hold it for me, I want to swim" I took it saying nothing. I saw crocodiles running inside the dam, rosemary took time under water then came to the surface and said, "come my love and swim together' Me: No. I saw crocodiles getting inside, so it is not safe. Come out now Rosemary, "I was afraid that they could attack her. **Rosemary:** 'crocodiles attacking me? Ha ha-ha laughing continues Crocodiles also afraid of me Nigel" she then took another dove inside water for over thirty minutes. She then came out undressed the other half of her body was in the water. I didn't ask why she was naked. She gave me a goodbye sign, and then went back inside for more minutes than the first time.

I kept staring hard in the water and began feeling dizzy. Her phone started ringing and saw it was a new number. **Me:** Hello. " "Yeah, Nigel, where arrived home its Patricia. Where are you?" He instantly put the phone call on hold. Prince and Patricia they come to Rosemary's funeral, really? Then I started to feel more excruciating dizzy. Then came a wind blowing from behind. I wanted to get off the bottom of the water and go a little way away, but the dizziness wouldn't let me go. The wind was getting stronger every second. Rosemary didn't come out from the dam. I knew that here comes trouble again. The police are looking for me obvious and U. K. team is here to mourn.... Oh God.

CHAPTER THIRTEEN

It is said that demons once felt that you are spiritually down when it comes to praying, you will dance according to their tunes. Devil can make sure that grace will never pick you until you are finished. I was one of those types of people who love Jesus but do not have him in their hearts, maybe that's why Rosemary was doing these strange things to me. But this day I remembered God in heaven, when I was in desperate time. I was lying on the rock and felt like I was having fever at first, and I kept getting hotter and hotter until I felt like I was growing to throw up. In addition, I felt dizzy, and my vision faded to black. But I was still conscious and having complete control over my body. This is where most people would sit down and then either their sight would come back or they would pass out. The wind was heavy and wanted to throw me in the dam. I took Rosemary's phone and dialed the number which Patricia had used to call me. It ranged for a while without being picked up then she picked up, "hello Patricia I am at the dam please help…" without finishing, it slipped and fell inside the dam.

I started crawling with on my stomach away to the dam. The rushing wind both with the dizziness halted. I stood up and started gazing at the dam and saw Rosemary coming out of the middle of the dam. The other half-way body was still in the water. "Nigel comes here, Daddy. I want to teach you how to swim," she said, waving her hand for me to come to where she was. I stared her hard saying nothing… without blinking so that my vision never disrupted. This time I won't say it confused me, the whole vision changed, and I lost my real image of site. Everything looked not clear and as I was going blind every second. The atmosphere changed into different dripping colors like rainbow hovers in ease and grace like, sniffing in the air laden sky. My visibility was near zero, even Rosemary was like she was far away, though I wiped my eyes but nothing changed. I started seeing myself floating in the air as I was astral traveling going to where Rosemary was. When I reached her, I went straight into her hands, which was cold. I looked home direction, and saw Patricia and Prince running towards us waving their hands to stop us, with few people to rescue me oh poor Nigel. When Rosemary saw them, she went underneath water with me and this was my last time to see outside. Rosemary kept on moving with me to where she seemed to know.

I was underwater because I was weightless, quiet soaring with the smallest amount of physical exertion. When we descended deeper down below, I was welcomed into an underwater world filled with amazing colors and beauty. Large crabs, fish and different water animals scuttling their way along and below us.

I had never seen these kinds of animals in their natural habitat. For me, I was in awe of what lies beneath the surface and how marine life comes in all kinds of shapes, sizes and colors, and lives in all kinds of the different environment, adapting to them perfectly. Hippos and crocodiles were giving us the way, and we were moving quickly. This was my first time seeing Rosemary in mermaid body. The other half body was Rosemary and the other half was a fishtail. Since I grew up, I heard about mermaids and couldn't believe those fairy tales. I thought maybe it was our elders ways to scare children not to play near water because they get drown, But today the real truth was in front of me. **Rosemary**: "Nigel, whatever you will see don't save it right!" I didn't answer her because I was afraid that once I open my mouth water will flood in. What surprised me is that I was breathing properly having this hidden mermaid ability.

Rosemary: "Nigel, for now, Patricia is the one holding your life. If anything bad happens to you don't blame me. You saw them coming running to stop us outside right. If they cry, I am going to lose you love." What? She was talking about me getting killed? By who? This was the moment I was most afraid, knowing that death is not far away. It was an emotional time, and though it's hard to talk about it. What are you talking about Rosemary? You are the one who brought me here. Now you want to kill me, what wrong have I done to deserve all this "I asked her with this fear of getting killed. **Rosemary:** "Shih! Quiet. We arrived. Please, Nigel do whatever they ask you to do. If you become rude, you will die. Respect and obedience is a guarantee here. Don't be rude, my boy. She left me and started going forth where there were other mermaids; they seemed both gentle and destructive. Underneath was now blue, which was refreshing. The water was cold. I could feel it around my face, but the whole body was being trapped in a flimsy layer of warm air that kept me snug. Air bubbles kept obscuring my view, but I could see everything. I remain paused at this place not knowing what to do... water was everywhere.

This place was more civilized and well organized than places I know ever exists on earth. Fish and mermaids kept going back and forth in front, top and behind me. They were types and types of mermaids, oh so this is how mermaids looks like?" They seemed not being bothered by my attention. I was really in love with this place which was evergreen and perfect. It was like my own paradise on earth, I will never forget the freshness of the water which was kissing my lips and those meandering islands gently through the pathways. My mind was a swirling vortex with these iridescent colors of beauty mother nature. They were small islands located nearby in different designs and shapes arranged in order. They were another place which was coming loud noise like a crèche or a hospital I don't know what to say.

From a distance appeared a young mermaid of golden hair which was shimmering and golden scales from an inch above her golf ball sized beady fish eyes, up over her head and down past her shoulders. Her skin was a steely grey, not shiny like scales; her nose was small and flattened with small nostrils. She was extremely beautiful than Rosemary. She floated all the way like a feather to where I was stationed. Her striking beauty made me fall in love with her. It came and held my hand and we went to a place where they were green loan and sat on it. She started talking in an unknown language, which was difficult to understand. After she saw that I did not understand her language, she started using signs for me to understand.

I was already in lusting mode on her also same to her; I saw by her strange actions of affirmation. One thing which was stopping me from proposing was the language barrier only. I differed from all of them. I looked everywhere maybe I could find Rosemary, but she was nowhere to be found. All I saw were women with breast and long hair. This injected fear in me that why these creatures are only women and what they would do to me as I was the only man. We stayed for a while and she kept doing funny things to make me laugh. She was friendly and caring. Soon she left me and came back within seconds holding a small bucket full of food. Quickly, I opened it and found out that it was only fresh fish which was coming blood. She picked one and started eating with her mouth open, some pieces falling out, and making disgusting noises. Arch... I took it from her and threw it away. Oh! Fundamentally disgusting, raw meat can contain a variety of harmful microorganisms or Raw or Trichinella, a parasitic worm. I thought maybe she wanted to cook it at first but my suspicions were not true. She became upset and started yelling at me with her language, then commanded me to eat them. I denied that food by shaking my head. She took another one and put it in on my mouth to eat but I did the same thing. I don't know how to explain how frustrated she becomes; she stood up circling me thrice and started coming to me with an angry long face. "Rosemary, Rosemary, help, it will eat me, "I screamed loudly. Immediately, I saw something coming so fast, slashing water sideways, then grabbed that young mermaid and chased her away. "Nigel, I told you to do whatever they tell you. Why do you not listen? You will die here, this is not home. Eat whatever they give you" she said and I don't know what she told that small mermaid and she disappeared. It seemed that many mermaids fears and respects Rosemary. It left me alone, and then started dozing off to sleep. This place was no sun; the sky was dark orange, and it was like a world of magic. I was asleep. Rosemary wake me up and sat next to me. "Nigel, I love you. What are you seeing on me now is the real me.

Also, when I am outside water, it's still real me? But now it's 100% Rosemary. Now, Patricia and Prince are crying outside the dam. My master is saying you must die because your relatives are crying, if they didn't cry you were supposed to live" she said wrapping my body with her cold-blooded seven-foot tail. The cold moves in only to meet the warmth of my blood, my defense against such a cold-blooded tail. I feel it wash over my skin, again and again, only to be met by the beat of my heart, again and again. Adrenaline floods my system. It pumps and beats like it's trying to escape. I think my heart will explode and my eyes are wide with fear. My body wants to either run fast for the safety but the question was where? This is not my territory or on the land, but I remain where I am. I can taste saliva thickening in my throat and beads of sweat trickling down my brow. **Me:** "So Rosemary, are you the one who will kill me?" **Rosemary:** "No, Nigel, why your relatives are crying, babe? Queen is saying you must die before tomorrow. "

About the Author

Paul kuipa is one of the greatest Zimbabwean upcoming greatest authors. His prophetic journey started a long time ago while he was still young, and now he is not stopping saving God's souls and furthering his kingdom. He grew up in a rural area and soon moved to stay in Harare where he finished his studies and started following his calling. He was born in Mutare, Dangamvura, one of Zimbabwe's oldest towns. Speaking about his author career of writing books, has has achieved some goals so far, and has written a few books, In Love With A Mermaid, The Life Of A Prophet, Pulling Down Curtains Of The Spirit Realm, My Name Is Eli, School Of Prophets, Saints And Sinners, Dreams And Their Interpretation etc. though some of the are already online in different sites include, Amazon, payhip, and Ibooks. Some of them are still to be published, I hope soon by God's grace his name will be heard as well as his books